I stared, awestruck, at the gems on display in the Tower of London. The gold, the diamonds, the sapphires, the emeralds, the silver. I turned to the guard standing nearby. "Are these jewels real?"

He wrinkled his nose as if he smelled something foul and looked down at me. "Yes, miss. After all, this is not Disney World."

I wanted to die of mortification. I heard snickers from the tour group behind me. Would I ever learn what to say and not to say in front of people?

"This isn't Disney World?" Kit whispered to me. "One look at the guard's Mickey Mouse–like ears, and I thought that's where we were!"

I couldn't help myself. I burst out laughing. The guard glared at me, but he had lost his power over me because of Kit's comment. I wanted to sling my arms around Kit's neck and thank him for coming to my rescue. But I couldn't do that.

As the group continued the tour, I avoided standing close to Kit. He was too cute, too English, too intimidating, too male, and too unexpectedly nice and funny. *I can't like him,* I warned myself. *He would be horrified by the real me. I would never be able to talk above a whisper if I liked him. I'd never be able to be myself. Don't like him!*

Year Abroad Trilogy

London: Kit & Robin

RACHEL HAWTHORNE

BANTAM BOOKS
NEW YORK · TORONTO · LONDON · SYDNEY · AUCKLAND

RL: 6, AGES 012 AND UP

LONDON: KIT & ROBIN
A Bantam Book / September 2000

Cover photography by Michael Segal.

Produced by 17th Street Productions,
an Alloy Online, Inc. company.
33 West 17th Street
New York, NY 10011.

ISBN: 0-553-49326-4

Visit us on the Web! www.randomhouse.com/teens

Published simultaneously in the United States and Canada

Bantam Books is an imprint of Random House Children's Books, a
division of Random House, Inc. BANTAM BOOKS and the rooster
colophon are registered trademarks of Random House, Inc. Bantam Books,
1540 Broadway, New York, New York 10036.

PRINTED IN THE UNITED STATES OF AMERICA

OPM   0 9 8 7 6 5 4 3 2 1

For Renee.
May you touch your dreams.

London:
Kit &
Robin

Prologue

From: U.S.Robin
Sent: Friday, September 1 . . . 8:03 P.M.
To: BritishKit
Subject: Me and London

Hey, Kit:

In less than twenty-four hours I'm gonna be in London! Is that the coolest thing or what?! I can't wait to meet you and your family. I can't wait for the first day of school! (Whoa—did I really just say that?? No one here in Mustang, Texas, would believe it!)

Thanks for offering to pick me up at the airport. Seven-thirty P.M. at Heathrow Airport, baggage claim. Here are my vital stats: short, blond hair, blue eyes, tallish, jeans, and a red down vest. Just look for the incredibly excited American! My two best buds will be with me too. It's gonna be so hard to say good-bye to them. Well, I'd better finish packing and then hit the sack.

—Robin Carter

P.S. Do you say "hit the sack" in England? Guess I'll find out soon enough!

One

Robin

TEEN, *SEVENTEEN, JANE, Mademoiselle.* All the mags said: *Be bold. Be brave. Girl power and all that. Ask him out. He'll like it.*

Yeah. Uh-huh. Right. They weren't talking about Jason Turner. Or me. Maybe all those articles about getting up the guts were for girls who didn't have any guts to start with. I'd always had too many guts.

Because asking out Jason Turner was the dumbest thing I'd ever done. It was pretty much the reason why I was on this airplane—and about to change my whole stupid life and my whole unsuitable self.

Okay, okay. Just because I asked out Jason and he turned me down (in front of everyone, mind you) didn't mean my life was stupid or that I should change everything about myself. But you have to

3

understand—I asked him out, like, *ten* times. Okay, maybe more like *twenty*. And he kept saying no. But I kept asking anyway, thinking I'd wear him down and he'd say yes.

Turned out I wore him down and he said no. Twenty times.

He didn't say the big, fat *no* (in front of everyone) until I got sort of pushy. And that was when I finally got the message. About how incredibly unappealing I was as a girl. *Uncouth* had been one of the words Jason used in his megaphone-esque *no*, actually. I had to look it up in the dictionary. *Uncouth* meant—

"Stop thinking about Jason!"

I turned to the left and stared at my co–best friend, Carrie Giovani. She was twisting her long, brown hair into a low bun. "How'd you know I was thinking about him?"

I heard a fake laugh to my right. Dana Madison, my other co–best friend, gently clasped my chin in her hand and turned me to face her. "You're always thinking about him! So cut it out and look out the window. We're almost there!"

I smiled. "Well, then move that head of yours outta the way so I can see!" The three of us had drawn straws, and Dana had won the window seat. Carrie had gotten second-best—the aisle. I was stuck in the middle. But being stuck between my two best buds for eleven hours wasn't so bad. Especially considering that I wouldn't see them—except for a few scattered weekend visits—for a year!

"Robin, we're serious," Carrie added. "We can always tell you're thinking about that jerk when you get quiet. Forget Jason! He thought he was so cool just because he moved from Dallas to Mustang. *Hello! Big whoop. You're* going to *London!* In, like, half an hour you're going to be on the soil of your heroine!"

Princess Diana's face floated into my mind. Carrie was right. I had to stop obsessing about Jason Turner right now. Why was I wasting my time thinking about that gorgeous, smart, funny, irresistible—

You're hopeless, I told myself. "Okay, okay. You guys caught me. I won't think about him once while I'm in London. I swear—"

The pilot cut me off as the overhead speaker buzzed on. "Ladies and gentlemen, this is Captain Ron speaking. We are beginning our final descent into Heathrow Airport."

"Yeehaw!" I shouted, then clamped my mouth shut. On this plane, which was flying direct from Dallas, Texas, there were a lot of loud women with big, blond hair and men in cowboy hats and really tight jeans. This was a *yeehaw* kind of environment.

But they didn't say *yeehaw* in London. Which was one of the main reasons I was heading there. Princess Diana didn't say *yeehaw* to express her

5

excitement. I wonder how she would have reacted to having a loudmouth tomboy from some tiny town in Texas idolizing her. She'd have probably been really nice about it and said something like, "How lovely." After all, the princess had been a true lady. The meaning of the word *refined*. She was exactly what I wanted to learn how to be.

So I had better remember to say "how lovely" in response to everything everyone in England said to me. Or I'd be laughed out of London the way I'd been laughed out of Mustang High School.

Carrie crowded against me to peek out the window, and I crowded against Dana. The three of us stared out, unable to speak as a million tiny, twinkling lights suddenly came into view. I had never seen anything like it before in my life.

For a moment I couldn't believe this was really happening. I pinched myself again—and felt it. So this wasn't a dream. I—Robin Jo Carter from bump-in-the-road Mustang, Texas—was actually about to arrive in the coolest of cities.

London!

I grabbed Carrie's hand and then reached for Dana's. "Can y'all believe I'm gonna spend a whole year in London?"

"I still can't believe you guys didn't pick Paris," Dana said, returning her attention to her *French for Travelers* handbook. The girl was a total Francophile, which meant she was really, really,

really into all things French. Paris was cool, of course, and so was Rome, which was where Carrie was heading, but nothing beat London. After all, Princess Di had lived there.

Before Carrie or I could wax on about why our cities were the coolest, the plane bumped through the air, and the pilot announced we were flying through a bit of turbulence, not to worry. My stomach almost dropped to the ground—which was still thousands of miles below. But the sensation only added to my excitement. I'd never been on a plane before. Heck fire! I'd never even been out of *Texas*. My dad was a farmer, a full-time, year-round job that didn't give my family many opportunities to travel.

"Don't worry about the bumpiness," Carrie reassured me. (She'd been on planes many times before.) "It's totally normal."

I smiled. "I don't mind a ton of bumpiness as long as I know I'm headed to London. Gosh, I owe y'all big time for this," I said to both of them as I pressed harder against Dana and strained to see if the tiny lights had turned into visible forms of the city.

"Remember how dead set against this your dad was?" Dana mused.

I suddenly envisioned Daddy, in his work overalls, hat, and big boots, telling me I could go on the program with his blessing. That had taken some doing. My mom had been reluctant too, but my daddy had been the absolute worst. My folks had grown up in tiny Mustang, Texas. They'd spent their honeymoon at Six Flags, for goodness sake, and the flags of Mexico, Spain, and France that snapped in the breeze at the entrance to the theme park was the closest they'd ever come to traveling abroad.

Carrie and Dana were from Mustang too, but they lived in *town*—not on a farm way out in the middle of nowhere, like I did. Carrie's parents were involved in the local theater and were really big into activism, like getting folks to vote and enter raffles. Carrie's mom was Mustang's liaison to the Year Abroad program (the Giovanis went to Italy for a vacation every year to visit their relatives). So the Giovanis worked on the Madisons, and both families worked on my mom, and then my mom worked on my dad, and suddenly I got the okay to go. Mr. Giovani had told my dad I'd return from London a sophisticated young woman. My daddy had said that was what he was afraid of—I was a farm girl, not Eliza Doolittle!

I knew who Eliza Doolittle was. Mustang High had put on the play two years ago. And I could really relate to the character. As a matter of fact, I sorta saw myself as a Texas Eliza Doolittle—thanks to the not-so-kind words of Jason Turner.

Yep, I was Eliza Doolittle, all right. Only a

little worse. I carried pigs around instead of flowers.

Returning to Mustang as a sophisticated young lady was exactly what I intended to do after my year abroad. More than anything I wanted to be elegant, reserved, and proper, like Princess Diana and the English girls I'd seen on TV and in the movies. After a year in London, I'd never again be the loud, brash big mouth who embarrassed herself all the time. I'd be a girl who I and others would approve of. And it was my English host "sister," Kit Marlin, who I intended to study and imitate.

"Daddy can't comprehend how embarrassing it is to be a farm girl," I said, trying to explain my parents. But as we all knew, sometimes you just couldn't explain adults. "I'm so *uncultured*. He doesn't understand that I want to be different from the way I am."

"I don't get that part either," Dana told me. "Why do you want to be someone you're not when who you are is so great?"

"Great?" I scoffed. "If I'm so great, then why wouldn't Jason Turner go out with me?"

Dana raised her finely arched eyebrows. "Because he's a jerk?"

Dana had short, chic red hair and the greenest eyes I'd ever seen. She looked like an aristocrat. I knew she couldn't understand why I hated coming across as though I'd just fallen off a turnip truck.

9

"*I* was the jerk," I said. "I've got a loud voice. I talk without thinking. I embarrassed Jason. I embarrassed myself. I've been embarrassing myself forever—without even knowing it. All the times I thought people were laughing with me, they were really laughing at me."

Dana shook her head. "I think you're making a big mistake to use this year abroad to become something you aren't." She leaned forward slightly. "You're just fine the way you are. Tell her, Carrie."

Carrie shrugged, making her dangling earrings jangle. Her olive complexion and dark hair made her look exotic. She credited her Italian heritage with what we called her *allure*. "I think her plan sounds like fun. We're supposed to use this year to experience new things. Stores, clothes, food—"

"Guys!" we all said at once, and laughed.

I definitely planned to experience guys. As soon as I lost my slow Texas drawl and learned to talk like a cultured person, I knew I'd have guys knocking on my door. No more *y'all* for me!

I leaned toward the window, practically smushing Dana against it.

"Come on." Dana unbuckled her seat belt. "This is your city. Let's switch seats."

"City! Not *town*. Incredible!" I knew I was being small townish by getting excited about a city, but I couldn't help myself. These last few minutes before the plane actually touched down would be my last as Texas Robin. Once those wheels hit the runway, I would be well on my way to becoming London Robin.

Dana and I giggled as we squeezed past each other. There wasn't a lot of room in an airplane. You most definitely did not want to sit by someone you didn't like for hours on end. I dropped into the window seat and quickly refastened my seat belt. I'd promised my daddy that I would follow all the rules. He was such a worrier.

I touched my fingers to the smooth glass and stared out the window. I desperately wanted to catch my first glimpse of London but could only see thick, white, billowing clouds. I wondered if Kit was already at the airport. Was she staring up at the white clouds, waiting to catch a glimpse of the plane?

Kit and I had e-mailed each other a couple of times. It was a little strange e-mailing someone I'd never met. I didn't really know what to say to her, so I kept the e-mails fairly brief. I didn't want to give too much away because I planned to alter my personality while I was in London, and I didn't want to confuse Kit.

Like me, Kit Marlin was an only child. I had always wanted a sister. Someone to share the house with. We could swap clothes, jewelry, perfume, and makeup. We could talk late into the night any night we wanted. I wouldn't have to wait for a sleep over.

11

I would have a year-round sleep over with my new sister.

It was going to be the most wonderful year of my life!

There was a wispy break in the clouds. Buildings, land—a mosaic of brown and green—and water came into view quickly and then disappeared. My breath hitched.

"Did you see that?" I asked breathlessly.

"I saw it," Dana and Carrie said at the same time.

"It was awesome," Dana told me.

I latched my gaze past the window, searching for another glimpse of the city I had dreamed about for months. The plane broke through the last barrier of clouds. I marveled at the domed roofs, spires, old buildings and new reaching toward the sky. And a castle. I could actually see Windsor Castle.

"Oh my gosh, y'all," I whispered in awe. "We're definitely not in Texas anymore."

After getting our luggage, we'd had to go through the passport inspectors and then the customs inspectors. I was beginning to think we'd never get out of the airport. After what seemed an eternity, I stood in the public lobby and waiting area with the backpack and laptop I'd carried on the plane plus my three pieces of luggage at my feet. The night before, I had tied bright purple ribbons around the handles so that I could find them quickly. Now I wished I hadn't been so efficient. I had way too much time to look around.

English accents surrounded me. People whizzed by, looking ever so sophisticated. I was struck dumb for the first time in my life. I was suddenly hit with reality and fear: I was in a foreign country, and my friends were about to abandon me! Carrie and Dana had a layover in London until tomorrow, so they were staying in a hotel. They would be so close, but so far away at the same time.

My stomach was tied up in one big knot tighter than the bows on my luggage. Standing here, waiting for Kit, was worse than waiting on the judges at the county fair to place ribbons on the winning livestock.

Carrie and Dana stood beside me. They had piled their bags on a nearby cart. Miss Lawrence, the YA sponsor, walked over to us.

"Did you get all your luggage?" she asked.

"Yes, ma'am," we answered in unison.

"Wonderful. As soon as Robin gets picked up, the rest of us will head to the hotel. I'm going to check on the best way to get there." She narrowed her gaze. "Stay put. You're not allowed to go off on your own until you've hooked up with your host family." She walked toward the glass doors at a brisk pace.

"Stay put?" Carrie retorted. "Like there's

some trouble we can get into before our host family picks us up that we can't get into after they pick us up?"

"She's responsible for us," Dana explained.

"What an important job! Fly around the world and drop off students." Carrie's voice dripped sarcasm. She had always been the most independent. I figured that happened when you had five brothers and one sister. Carrie was accustomed to taking care of herself.

"If it wasn't for Miss Lawrence, Robin wouldn't be here at all," Dana pointed out. "Her parents wouldn't let her fly all the way to London by herself. Isn't that right, Robin?"

Dana was Miss Logical, always watching out for the underdog.

"Right," I replied, distracted.

Where is Kit? I wondered. My host sister should have already been here. I glanced at my watch. Somewhere over the Atlantic Ocean, I had set it to London time. *Over the Atlantic.* I'd even slept over the Atlantic. Not bad for a small-town girl.

"Where's your host family?" Carrie asked.

"Only Kit is coming." I searched the crowd like I knew who I was looking for. But I only had a vague idea of what Kit looked like. In the few e-mails we had exchanged, we'd never gotten around to exchanging pictures. I knew Kit was tall. She had blond hair and blue eyes, like me. I also knew that Kit and I would get along well. After all,

14

I had a great-aunt named Kit, so I saw that as a good sign. It made being thousands of miles from home seem not quite so scary.

"So far I'm not impressed with your host sister," Dana said. "She should have been here on time. She must have known you'd be nervous."

"I'm not nervous," I assured her. *Terrified* was a better word. *Frightened*. *Scared*. Either of those would work too.

There were so many people. They all looked confident. They spoke briskly, walked briskly. They knew where they were going. What had I been thinking to want to travel thousands of miles from home? The airport was as big as Mustang.

"Okay, listen," Carrie began, and I turned my attention to my friend. Carrie always had a plan. And she always talked with her hands drawing pictures in the air. She said it was the Italian in her blood.

"We have one day together in London tomorrow," Carrie continued. "What do we want to do?"

"Something touristy," Dana replied. "I promised Mom that I'd send her a postcard from London."

Carrie smiled. "Tower of London? We can take a gander at the crown jewels. Maybe they even have some that we can try on. What do you think, Robin?"

"Sounds good," I murmured. I started searching the crowds more diligently, my worry increasing. If

15

my host sister didn't show up, I would have to go to the hotel with Miss Lawrence. Not a good way to begin my year of adventure.

Where in the heck was Kit? She'd written that she'd wear a red sweater.

My wandering gaze slammed to a halt as I spotted a red sweater. Then my hopes sank deeper than a Texas oil well. I was looking at a guy leaning against the far wall. A very cute guy.

I barely managed to tear my eyes off him to look around for another red sweater. But I could feel the guy's eyes on me. I sneaked a glance back at him. He *was* looking at me. He was tall, with blond hair that fell across his brow.

He shoved himself away from the wall and ambled hesitantly toward me. He stopped in front of me, angled his head, and narrowed incredible blue eyes. He looked like someone who was trying to solve an extremely difficult problem.

"Red vest, short, blond hair, blue eyes, with two American friends—are you by any chance Robin Carter?"

I froze. His elegantly spoken words slammed into me with the force of a stampeding bull. They were the exact words I'd written in my e-mail when I told Kit what to look for. Horror swept through me.

Kit Marlin was a *guy?*

16

TWO

Robin

KIT MARLIN HAD the most cultured voice I'd ever heard—warm and gentle, sort of like Hugh Grant's. Mine was more like a herd of cattle, which was exactly how Jason Turner had described it.

My mouth grew dry, and my chin tingled. I thought I might be ill. No, no, Princess Diana would never have thrown up in the middle of an airport.

I swallowed to get rid of the stuffed-cotton feel in my mouth. *Remember, you're in London now. Speak like Princess Di.* "I was expecting a female person," I said formally, in a very low voice to disguise my accent.

He leaned forward slightly. "Sorry?"

For what? I wondered. *Keeping me waiting?*

Then it dawned on me. That wasn't what he meant. I'd watched Hugh Grant in enough movies to realize that Kit meant, *Excuse me? What? Come again?*

I cleared my throat and said a little louder, "I was expecting a female person."

He smiled warmly. The most beautiful, welcoming smile I'd ever seen. "Kit is short for Christopher."

My scared-spitless smile evaporated as the reality hit me. Not only didn't I have an English sister to study and imitate, but I had to live in the same house with a guy for the first time in my life. I mean, I'd lived with my daddy, but that didn't count. He was a father. Kit was a . . . Well, Kit was a *guy!*

Sure, he was English and he was cute—to-die-for cute—but he was still a guy, and we'd be sharing accommodations!

If Jason Turner from no-big-deal Dallas thought I was a hillbilly, what was Kit Marlin going to think once he got to know the real me?

"Will you please excuse me a moment while I converse with my companions?" I asked Kit in a low voice.

He furrowed his brow. "Pardon?"

I reined in my impatience. I was certain that talking in a low voice would work once we got out of the bustling airport. Raising my voice just a little bit, ever mindful to keep my words clipped and even, I repeated, "Will you please excuse me a moment while I converse with my companions?"

"Oh, right," he said, nodding. "I'll watch your baggage."

Walking like I was balancing a book on the top of my head, I escorted Dana and Carrie to an area out of earshot. With my back to Kit, I contorted my face into an expression of hopeless despair. As much as I wanted to, I couldn't very well scream in the middle of the airport. "What am I going to do? He's a guy!"

"A cute guy," Carrie pointed out. "And that is so totally not fair. Your first night in London, and a dream guy walks right into your life."

"You're missing the point here! Didn't you hear him talk? He's too English. What do I do now? How am I gonna live in the same house with him? He's gonna think I'm a freak if he hears how I talk and sees how I act." I knew I was rambling, something I did when I was totally nervous—and at that moment I was more nervous than I'd ever been in my entire life.

"He won't think you're a freak," Dana assured me. "He'll like you just like we do."

I shook my head fiercely. "No, no, he won't. Can I stow away with one of you guys and go to Paris or Rome?"

Carrie put her hand comfortingly on my shoulder. "Hey? Aren't you dare-me-to-do-anything Robin?"

"I've only ever lived with my parents," I blurted out. Why couldn't they see what a disaster this was? "Don't dare me to live with a guy!"

"I've got five brothers," Carrie reminded me. "All you have to worry about is making sure that you get a good heaping amount of food on your plate before he sits down to eat because guys wolf down everything in sight. And you just need to check the toilet seat because they always leave it up. Always. It's disgusting."

"I can't do this," I insisted. "He was supposed to be a girl. Kit is a stupid name for a guy."

"As in Kit Carson?" Dana asked.

I glowered at her.

Dana shrugged. "I'm just saying . . . he seems okay with you being a girl. So you can handle this, Robin."

I glanced over my shoulder. Kit was watching me. He quickly looked away.

Carrie leaned close and whispered in my ear, "And he is so totally hot."

I glared at Carrie. "That's one of the things that makes this so hard."

But neither Dana nor Carrie was listening to my pleas for understanding. Instead their eyes were flashing silent *dare yous*. Sometimes it's not a good thing to have friends who know your weakness. I gave a brisk nod. "All right. I can do this. It's not a whole year. It's just a whole school year, which is what . . . one hundred and eighty days?" Wasn't that how Henry VIII counted the time he spent with his wives before he beheaded them—in days instead of years?

"You can do it," Carrie assured me.

"But you're going to have to stop whispering," Dana told me. "And the formal talk? Where did that come from? *Companions?* My grandmother has a *companion*. We're *friends*."

Carrie nodded. "I have to agree with Dana on this one. You sound too bizarre." She looked past me to where Kit was standing. "He, on the other hand, sounds just like Hugh Grant." She sighed dreamily. "You are so lucky!"

I felt anything except lucky, but I knew that Dana and Carrie were right. I had to stay. Convincing my parents had been a difficult task. If I changed plans now and went to Paris or Rome, they'd have a cow and tell me to come home.

"I'll cut back on the formal words, but not the low voice." I hated to admit it, but *female person* had been a little out there now that I thought about it.

"Oops, there's Miss Lawrence waving at the door. We've gotta go," Carrie said. She gave me a tight hug. "You're gonna do just fine."

I nodded, blinking back the tears stinging my eyes.

Dana hugged me fiercely and kissed my cheek. "Don't cry yet. We're still in the same city, and we'll see you tomorrow." She drew back and smiled. "And tomorrow night we'll all cry when we say good-bye."

Carrie grabbed Dana's arm. "Come on. Let's see if we can talk Miss Lawrence into taking us to a pub tonight."

"She's not going to take us to a pub," practical Dana responded.

"Simply for the cultural experience," Carrie assured her with a laugh.

"Y'all be careful," I called softly after them as they hurried to the cart holding their luggage. So softly that I didn't think they heard me. But I couldn't risk calling out, couldn't take a chance that Kit would hear my real voice.

I watched them say good-bye to Kit before pushing the cart toward the door. I felt like my lifeline was cut when the doors closed behind them.

I wanted to scream, *Wait, take me with you!*

But I had come here to change my screaming ways.

I pasted a smile on my face and walked toward waiting Kit.

I tried not to stare at Kit as he pulled my larger bags into the parking garage. I had my small bag, my laptop, and my backpack. Thank goodness my luggage had wheels. I never would have been able to haul it through the airport otherwise.

"I'm terribly sorry about making you wait so long," Kit said. "But I made the same mistake you did. I expected you to be a guy. Robin as in Robin Hood. I stood there for the longest time looking for a chap in a red vest."

Great! Now he's thinking of me as a boy.

In a low, twang-free voice I said, "I expected you to be a girl, as in my great-aunt Kit."

He paled and quickened his step.

Great start we're off to here, I thought glumly.

He came to a stop beside a black sedan. "Well, here we are. I'll put your things in the boot."

The boot? What was he talking about?

He opened the trunk. I felt like such a fool. "Oh, you mean the—"

My loud southern voice echoed around me. Thank goodness he'd just ducked his head into the trunk to shift some stuff around, so he didn't hear me. He grunted as he lifted my first suitcase. With a thud it landed in the trunk—the boot.

He rubbed his arm and stared at me. "Blast it all! What have you got in there? It must weigh ten stone."

Ten stone? Did he think I'd packed rocks?

They obviously had different words for things over here. I was going to have to remember that.

He obviously hadn't expected me to tell him what was in my suitcase because he went back to arranging my luggage inside the boot. He had broad shoulders. I didn't have any trouble imagining him working my daddy's fields.

I shivered because of the chill in the air. It was

ninety-eight degrees when I left Texas. I'd felt silly carrying a coat into the Dallas airport, but I was glad I had it now.

"Come on. Let's get you inside where it's a bit warmer," he said. He slammed the trunk closed and walked around to the left side of the car.

Panic surged through me as he unlocked the driver's-side door and held it open for me. I shook my head briskly and stated in a level voice, "I'm not driving."

He furrowed his brow and took a step toward me. "Pardon?"

"I'm not driving," I repeated a little more loudly, trying to keep my voice evenly clipped.

He gave a quick laugh. I liked his smile and the way his blue eyes twinkled.

"Of course you're not. You're sixteen, right?"

I nodded.

"You have to be seventeen to drive over here." He tilted his head slightly. "This is the passenger side."

I eased up slightly like I was approaching a cantankerous bull. I peered inside. No steering wheel.

I felt my face turn bright red. I grimaced and looked at him. "I forgot that you drive on the wrong side of the road here."

He laughed again. "It's you Americans who drive on the wrong side."

I almost barked out my laughter. Wouldn't he

find that charming? The way I brayed like a donkey.

I climbed into the car and took a deep breath. He got behind the steering wheel and started the car. This was weird, sitting on the driver's side without a steering wheel. I felt like I needed to wrap my hands around something, namely a steering wheel, but since there wasn't one in front of me, I balled up my hands and put them on my lap.

Whoa, boy! my mind screamed as he pulled into the left lane of the highway. Even though I knew he was going to do it, my reflexes kicked in. I stiffened and reached for a brake that wasn't on my side of the car.

He chuckled. "I suppose it's a bit strange— driving on the right side of the road for a change."

Only he wasn't on the right side. He was on the left side, so he was on the wrong side! I wanted to yell at him. Instead I glanced out the window at the gray sky.

"Does driving on the motorway make you nervous?" he asked.

I jerked my head around and looked at him. Was he talking about the highway we were driving on? He had to be. "No," I answered succinctly. *No* was a good, safe word with no extra syllables to accidentally draw out.

"Did you have a good flight?" he asked.

"Yes." Another safe word.

25

He cast a quick glance my way before turning his attention back to the highway. The motorway? He furrowed his brow. "I suppose it was a long flight coming all the way from Texas, as you were."

Silence. Was I supposed to respond to that? I didn't hear a question.

"My mum should have dinner ready by the time we get home," he told me. "The drive's a half hour. To give you a sense of where Hampstead is in London, it's about twenty minutes or so from Buckingham Palace."

I was still on *mum*. Wasn't that a flower used in homecoming corsages? Not that I'd ever had one, but I'd heard rumors.

"I think she's planning on a bit of bubble and squeak for tonight." He darted a quick glance my way. "Do you like that?"

What in tarnation was he talking about? I was getting more confused by the minute. He'd mentioned supper, but that couldn't be food. It had to be a game. That's what it was. We were going to play some sort of game to get better acquainted. His question required only a one-word answer, and that's all I was going to give him. "Yes."

"Oh, good. Mum will be pleased to hear that. She wasn't quite sure what to cook."

My stomach roiled. Bubble and squeak *was* food! Oh no. I'd told him that I liked it, so I'd have to eat it now—whatever the heck it was.

"So where are your friends going to school this year?" he asked.

"Paris and Rome."

"The one with the dark hair . . . her name would be?" he prodded.

I closed my eyes on a silent sigh. In my shock over his gender, I hadn't even bothered to introduce my friends. He probably thought I was the rudest person west of the Atlantic. My parents had raised me better than that. I opened my eyes. "Carrie."

"And she's the one going to?"

"Rome."

He smiled slightly. "And the girl with the short red hair?"

"Dana."

He nodded. "So she must be going to Paris. I feel rather like Sherlock Holmes with that deduction." He released what sounded like a nervous laugh. "It won't be much longer now."

I stared out the window. He was so formal and polite that he was scaring me to death. The longer we drove, the queasier my stomach got, and it didn't have anything to do with the speed of the car and the way he had to keep swerving in and out of traffic. I was going to a new house. A house I would live in for a whole year. A house I would live in for a whole year with this guy.

My stomach was knotting up so tightly that I didn't know how I'd eat supper. I wanted to ask him what bubble and squeak was, but then I'd have to confess that I had lied earlier, and wouldn't I look stupid?

A heavy silence wedged its way between us. I wanted to fill it with questions. I had at least a hundred. Was his mother like Queen Elizabeth? Not with the crown, of course, but regal? Was I supposed to salute his dad? Curtsy? Did they ever eat regular food like hamburgers and barbecued chicken?

I opened my mouth to ask Kit what his folks were like, but I didn't know if that was proper in England. I snapped my mouth closed.

It was better if we drove in silence anyway. After all, I didn't want him to ask *me* any more questions.

I couldn't imagine what his reaction would be if Mr. English City Boy learned that I had pet pigs and won the last hog-calling contest at the county fair.

Three

Robin

"MARVELOUS! I'VE ALWAYS wanted a daughter," Mrs. Marlin said as she hugged me.

I was having a hard time believing that I was standing inside a house in London. When Kit had pulled the car to a stop in front of the house, I could only stare. Brightwell Street was a row of two-story brick buildings lined up side by side like soldiers. The house looked narrow from the front, but inside it seemed larger. *Well laid out,* my daddy would say.

"Haven't I always said that, Nickie?" Mrs. Marlin asked. "That I'd like to have a daughter."

"Indeed you have, love," Mr. Marlin said as he stood smiling beside his wife.

Tall, with wavy, blond hair, Mr. Marlin reminded me a lot of Kit. Mrs. Marlin, on the other hand, was short and round, with black hair peppered with silver.

"We must not have paid much attention to the papers that they sent us, eh, Kit?" Mr. Marlin asked. His smile grew broader as he leaned toward me like he wanted to impart a national secret. "We thought you were a lad."

"I explained that to her, Dad," Kit said.

The heat of embarrassment scalded my face. Okay, so everyone had made an idiotic mistake. I wanted to forget it.

Mrs. Marlin slipped her arm through mine. "Let's give you a quick tour so you'll feel completely at home here. After all, this is your home now."

My home! Omigosh. A wave of homesickness washed over me. Staying here was quickly becoming a reality.

Although the downstairs area had a different feel to it that I couldn't quite identify—old English charm, maybe—it wasn't that much different from my house in Mustang. Except all the walls had flowered wallpaper on them. All the walls. At home we only had wallpaper in the kitchen and bathrooms.

A swinging door separated the kitchen from the dining room on one side of the house. No breakfast area like we had at home. A huge living room sat in the center of everything. Mr. Marlin's office was to the side. Kit's parents' bedroom was at the back. My parents' bedroom was at the back of the house, and my dad did all his paperwork in the room next door. Of course, his office didn't have leather books lining the bookshelves like this one. He had farm manuals and tattered farm-supply catalogs.

"It's a very nice house," I said quietly, politely.

Mrs. Marlin beamed. "Thank you, dear. And now, my prized garden."

I wondered what kind of vegetables she grew as we stepped through French doors onto a pebbled patio. Beyond, I could see flowers lining the house and trestles with ivy clinging and weaving its way up. Mrs. Marlin must have been referring to her flower garden. There wasn't anything else in the yard except for a small white gazebo and some stone benches.

"We're quite pleased with the garden," Mrs. Marlin told me. "Kit helped his father make the gazebo for my birthday a few years back. I think it really adds to the beauty of the garden."

Garden. Yard. They had to be calling the yard a garden even though they were mostly growing grass. I felt like these people were speaking a foreign language. But Mrs. Marlin was completely elegant and regal as she daintily pointed to her flowers. Her speech was refined and proper. And soft without being a whisper.

I can learn from her, I thought. *I can study her and imitate her proper, sophisticated ways. Then I'll be exactly what I want to be.*

31

"Tell us about yourself, dear," Mrs. Marlin prodded.

I swallowed the knot rising in my throat as we strolled back into the house. Mr. Marlin and Kit were dogging our heels. I felt like I was walking to my execution. What could I tell them about myself that wouldn't make me sound like a country bumpkin? My mind was in an unnatural state—it was absolutely blank.

"We're your family now, dear," Mrs. Marlin said. "So you mustn't be shy. What sort of things do you like?"

I smiled at the simple question as the answer popped into my head. "I really like Ricky Martin."

Mrs. Marlin's face brightened. "Oh, so you have a boyfriend back home."

I stared at her. She was joking, right?

Kit cleared his throat. "Mum, Ricky Martin is a pop star."

His mother blushed. "Oh, of course. I probably knew that."

No, she didn't, I realized. Imitating Mrs. Marlin might turn me into a proper *nerd.*

"Although I'm sure Robin *does* have a boyfriend back home," Kit added.

Now I stared at him. *That* was unexpected. Why would anyone think *I* had a boyfriend anywhere?

"Come along, dear," Mrs. Marlin said. "I'll show you your room. It's on the first floor."

I watched her head up the stairs. The woman was insane. I was going to live a whole year with a crazy woman. Hadn't she said my room was down here?

"Go on," Kit said behind me, nearly making me jump out of my skin.

"She said my room was on the first floor," I explained in my low, twang-free voice.

"It is," Kit assured me.

"But she's going to the second floor," I muttered.

Kit shook his head and grinned. "She's going to the first floor." He pointed at his feet. "This is the ground floor."

I raised my finger toward his mother. "And that's the first floor?"

He nodded.

Great! I was going upstairs to the first floor. That made no sense.

"Nickie! Will you and Kit bring up Robin's things, please?" Mrs. Marlin called down in a lovely singsong voice.

I caught up with her at the top of the stairs.

"Here you are, dear," Mrs. Marlin said.

I stepped into the coziest room. The walls were decorated with pale lilac wallpaper adorned with bouquets of lilies. The room had a small fireplace, although no fire burned in the hearth. Beside the fireplace was a four-poster bed with a lavender lace canopy.

"I'm ever so glad you turned out to be a

lass," Mrs. Marlin whispered conspiratorially. "I wasn't quite certain how a lad would take to this room."

"It's wonderful," I murmured, breathtaken. A small TV sat on a little table in the corner. It looked new, and I wondered if they'd bought it just for my visit.

The window had a violet padded bench seat beneath the windowsill. Perfect for curling up and looking out on London. Simply perfect.

"Kit's room is directly across the hall," Mrs. Marlin told me.

Not so perfect.

"You'll share the bathroom," Mrs. Marlin added.

Absolutely imperfect.

I stepped farther into the room. A small desk sat near the window. Above it on the wall hung a framed poster of the Dallas Cowboys. "They're not English," I blurted out.

"Kit put that up," Mrs. Marlin explained. "He thought it would make our new American guest from Texas less homesick."

He did? Hmmm. Maybe Kit wasn't quite the staid and proper guy that I thought he was.

If only Kit were a girl. I could throw myself at a girl's mercy and plead with her. *Help me! Change me! Make me just like you!*

But a guy? Way too embarrassing.

Especially one who lived right across the hall.

*   *   *

I was probably seriously suffering from jet lag, but I was too excited and too nervous to close my eyes for a second. So, I unpacked my bags. I placed my neatly folded clothes into drawers scented with lavender sachets. Hung my sweaters in a closet that smelled of cedar. Mrs. Marlin had told me to freshen up a bit before dinner—which would be in one hour.

What did that mean? Freshen up. On the farm it meant wash the dirt off your hands and the dust off your face, brush the tangles out of your hair. But this was London. And as I was quickly learning, the same words meant different things over here.

Boy, howdy. Freshen up. They'd given me an hour to do it. It had to mean dress up.

I was certain it did. Mrs. Marlin had said she was making a traditional English meal to welcome me. Was that a fancy meal? It had to be. Like I saw in the movies. The long table, the flickering candles, ten forks, and a dozen knives. Formal.

I had brought one formal gown. Should I wear it? Was it that kind of a dinner? Dinner, not supper. It even sounded fancy.

I needed some serious help.

I went to the phone on the small, dainty desk and dialed the hotel where Carrie and Dana were staying. The ringing took me by surprise—short, quick staccato bursts. When the hotel clerk answered, I asked for their room. I sat carefully in the elegant chair, fearful of breaking it. I listened to the phone ring, ring, ring. *They must have talked Miss Lawrence into taking them to a pub,* I thought glumly. A cultural experience.

How's this for a cultural experience? I have no idea what I'm doing here!

I hung up and began to pace. I desperately wanted to call my mom, but we'd agreed to call only once a week to cut down on the expense of this trip. Calling about what to wear to dinner seemed trivial. I had no idea what other crisis would erupt before the week was out—and I might really need my mom then.

Better to save the phone call. I could set up my laptop and e-mail my mom, but she would be busy with chores right now. It might be hours before I got a reply, and that would be way too late.

Admit it, Carter. You are totally alone here, and you don't know how to do the simplest things!

How countrified is that?

A bundle of nerves, I plopped onto the bed, fell onto my back, and flung out my arms in hopeless frustration. I stared at the lace canopy. The web of tiny threads made me feel trapped.

How in the heck am I gonna handle the first day of school the day after tomorrow? I can't even handle going to dinner. How am I gonna talk to anyone if I have to hide my accent?

Things were really getting bad. Now I was rambling to myself. Why couldn't Kit have been a girl so he could have helped me out? He'd probably already changed into his clothes for dinner. How much trouble was it for a guy? Slacks, shirt, jacket.

"Robin!" Mr. Marlin called. "Dinner's almost ready!"

Omigosh! I wasn't ready. What had I been doing for an hour? Worrying. That's what! What had it gotten me? Nothing.

I grabbed a black skirt and a lacy white blouse from the closet. If I worked really quickly, I could make myself presentable for dinner.

I felt like a total fool.

No candles. Only one fork, one knife, one spoon. No long, elegant table. No one dressed in finery.

Everyone else had done exactly as Mrs. Marlin suggested. They had simply freshened up. They hadn't changed clothes. Kit was still wearing jeans and his red sweater.

"You look lovely, dear," Mrs. Marlin said as she passed me the leg of lamb.

I wished the floor would open up and swallow me whole. Or better yet, where was a good tornado when I needed one?

"That's the first thing I'd do after a long flight," Kit announced.

I looked at him, sitting across the table from me. "What?"

"Change into some other clothes," he answered almost innocently, but his eyes twinkled with mischief.

Did he honestly think that was the reason I had changed clothes, or was he making fun of me?

"Dad, you need to pass Robin the bubble and squeak. She fancies it," Kit explained.

"Fancy that," Mr. Marlin murmured as he picked up a bowl. "Have you eaten many British foods?"

With trepidation, I took the bowl and peered inside. Cabbage and potatoes. I almost laughed. Cabbage wasn't my favorite, but I could tolerate it, especially when the alternative was admitting to a lie.

"No," I said in a low voice as I scooped a heaping onto my plate.

All three Marlins leaned toward me and said, "Pardon?" at the same time. I almost choked, trying so hard not to laugh. I was definitely going to have to speak a little more loudly.

"No," I repeated, and they all settled back into their chairs.

"Well, then, you're in for a lovely treat. Maude made trifle for dessert," Mr. Marlin told me.

"Mum doesn't make it often," Kit added. "It's a lot of trouble to cook."

The heat warmed my face. "You shouldn't have gone to any trouble," I told Mrs. Marlin.

"Nonsense, dear. Kit is just giving me a hard

time because I only make it for special occasions, and he'd gobble it down every night if he could," Mrs. Marlin said.

Watching the refined way that Kit ate, I couldn't imagine him gobbling anything. He ate precisely, his fork in his left hand, his knife in his right. Glancing around the table, I realized I was the only one who cut the meat with my right hand and then put the fork in my right hand to bring it to her mouth. Were they all lefties, or was this a British ritual?

"So tell us a bit about Texas," Mr. Marlin urged me.

I almost choked on my lamb. I drank some milk, anything to dislodge the food stuck in my throat. I glanced across the table. Kit studied me as if I were something from another planet. I couldn't tell these classy people that I came from a farm, had pigs and goats, and could milk a cow really well.

"Mustang is a small town," I told them, glancing nervously around the table. "Everyone knows everyone."

Relatively small words, low voice. I hadn't detected any twang in my speech.

"The school we'll be going to is rather like that," Kit explained. "Only those students preparing to go on to the university will be there."

He looked like he expected me to say something. But what?

"What do you do for fun?" Mr. Marlin inquired.

"Fun?" I repeated.

"Yes. In America. What do you do?" he repeated.

Mud runs. Tractor pulls. Rodeos. Wouldn't that impress the heck out of them?

"Movies," I responded quietly.

"What sort of movies?" Mr. Marlin asked.

He wasn't going to let me get off with a one-word answer. What was he? A lawyer?

"Probably the same sort of movies that we watch, Dad," Kit said as he reached for some bread. "I don't imagine that the kids over there are that much different from us over here."

"That's what we're supposed to find out this year, isn't it?" Mr. Marlin asked. "We share our culture, she shares hers."

"Speaking of culture," I said quietly. "I promised my friends that I'd meet them at the Tower of London tomorrow. Is there a bus stop near here?"

"The tube would be better," Kit told me. "You can catch it right down the street."

I stared at him. The tube? Why did sliding down water-park rides flash through my mind?

Mrs. Marlin chuckled. "You look confused, Robin."

"Uh, no," I lied, determined to make this year work if it killed me. "Which end of the street?"

"Kit will take you tomorrow," Mrs. Marlin said.

Kit and I both groaned low and then jerked our gazes to each other. Okay, so Dana had been wrong.

He wasn't any more thrilled with me than I was with him.

He slid his gaze to his mother. "You mean just walk her to the end of the street?"

"No, I mean take her to the Tower. For goodness sake, we can't have her getting lost after only one day. You need to show her how to use the tube and get around a bit. Tomorrow will be perfect for that, don't you think?"

Kit's gaze darted back to me. I knew he wanted to say no. It was in his eyes. Instead he nodded.

"Sure, Mum. I didn't have any plans," he muttered with an edge to his voice. It was sharp enough that I could have used it to cut the lamb.

"I'm glad that's settled. Robin, you must realize this is your home. Just let us know what you need," Mrs. Marlin told me.

I need to feel sophisticated. I need a sister, not a brother who has the most intense blue eyes I've ever seen.

"Anything. Anything at all," Mr. Marlin said. "By the way, what does your father do for a living?"

My heart slammed against my ribs. I felt Kit watching me as I slowly chewed the broccoli, taking a moment to collect my thoughts. I loved my dad, but I didn't want to tell these people he was a farmer, a small-town farmer at that.

"Dad, I thought I heard the car make a strange rumbling noise on the way back from the airport," Kit declared.

I didn't remember hearing anything, but then,

I'd been in semishock at discovering I had a brother instead of a sister.

"Mmmm," Mr. Marlin mumbled. "I'll look into it tomorrow."

Kit gave me a little wink. So Brits lied too. I wanted to thank Kit for steering the subject away from me. He seemed to realize I didn't like talking about myself because he began asking his dad questions about his plans for the week. And when he was finished with his dad, he started asking his mom questions.

I sat there, my stomach settling, so I was actually able to eat. And I thought the food might stay down. I loved listening to their accents. I had a hard time keeping my eyes off Kit. He was amazing to look at. I wanted to brush the lock of blond hair off his brow and watch it fall back into place. He had the cutest smile, a little on the shy side.

I thought about the poster in my room. About him explaining Ricky Martin to his mother. He wanted me to feel at home. And now he'd cleverly put a stop to the inquisition so I could relax.

He was much kinder and more thoughtful than I'd originally realized. And so incredibly hot looking.

How was I going to be able to sleep with him right across the hall?

Four

Kit

THE NEXT MORNING I rolled over in bed and slapped off the buzzing alarm. I squinted at the red numbers on my clock. 7:20 A.M. I groaned. It was my last day before school started up again, and I'd planned to sleep until noon. Why had I set the alarm?

Ah, right. The American.

I'd promised to take her and her friends on their tour of the Tower. What a drag that would be with soft-spoken, reserved Robin!

I flung myself onto my back and glared at the ceiling. Where was the brash American brother that I'd expected to be living with me when I had begged Mum and Dad to host a foreign-exchange student?

Robin was so prim, proper, and reserved—utterly boring!

I had figured that anyone who went on the Year Abroad program had to be gutsy, but Robin was more like a timid mouse waiting for the cat to pounce. She talked in such a quiet voice that I constantly had to ask her to repeat herself. *I might have to get a hearing aid for the year.*

As if that wasn't bad enough, she acted like her face would crack if she smiled.

How was I supposed to learn to loosen up and let go from Robin Carter? I had been counting on my American "bro" to help me figure out the best way to break up with Brooke and still remain friends with her. It had to be an American experience because actors in Hollywood seemed to have great success at doing it. I really didn't want to hurt Brooke. She was a lovely girl, but she was rushing our relationship along like it was a train going downhill without brakes.

We'd gone on two dates before she left for holiday two months ago. She had spent the summer touring the continent, sending me e-mails from different countries. I had thought it would be exciting to hear of her adventures. Instead I discovered she was scared of everything: foreigners, trains, eating ethnic food. She hated doing anything new and complained about anything unfamiliar.

She wasn't at all what I wanted in a girlfriend. I wanted someone who dared to take chances, who wasn't afraid of her shadow, who was willing to experience new things.

I furrowed my brow. Maybe I was judging Brooke too harshly. E-mail couldn't always convey a person's true personality. I thought about Robin's e-mail. She had certainly sounded enthusiastic and excitable. Exclamation marks everywhere. She hadn't spoken one exclamation-mark sentence since I'd met her at the airport. She was incredibly boring. Not at all what I'd expected—not to mention that she was a "female person."

So maybe the real Brooke was the girl I'd dated a couple of times. I hadn't meant to become her steady so quickly, but based on her letters over the summer, I realized she thought we were a hot item. I decided I should probably give her a chance.

Brooke wasn't supposed to get back from holiday until late tonight. I wouldn't be able to see her until we arrived at school tomorrow morning. Maybe I'd just read the tone in her letters wrong.

Well, I would have to worry about that tomorrow. I threw off the blankets and sat up in bed. Right now I had to get through what promised to be a really dull day in my as usual dull life!

I needed to hit the shower. Maybe the hot water beating on me would cheer me up. Not likely, but you never knew.

I knew seeing Robin certainly wouldn't cheer me. I had so looked forward to having a sibling, but not one who was so meek and mild mannered that she blended in with the wallpaper.

Wearing nothing but my underwear, I dragged myself into the hall—and stopped dead in my tracks.

Robin stood in the hallway—wearing nothing but her bra and panties!

My mouth dropped open. My eyes widened. The heat of embarrassment scalded my face. But my feet wouldn't move.

She stared at me. I stared at her.

Then she shrieked and darted into her room, slamming the door.

I rushed into my room, closed the door, and leaned against it. Right. That was embarrassing.

A grin spread across my face. But also incredibly funny! At least I'd finally managed to get an exclamation mark out of her.

Obviously Robin wasn't used to sharing a bathroom with someone of the opposite sex either. With my parents' bedroom downstairs, I was accustomed to living alone upstairs.

I dropped back my head. Robin definitely had cute curves. Truthfully, I hadn't seen anything that I wouldn't have seen if she were wearing a bikini. I just hadn't expected to ever see her in a bikini—at least not in my hallway. That had made the moment seem so personal, so intimate.

It shouldn't have because I didn't even like her. I chuckled low. At least I hadn't had any trouble hearing her shriek. Maybe I should suggest she think of me standing in the hall in my underwear whenever she needed to talk. Maybe then she would talk loud enough that I could hear her.

I combed my fingers through my hair and took a deep breath. I needed to tell her that she could have the shower first.

I grabbed my jeans off a nearby chair and jerked them on. Then I slipped a T-shirt over my head. This time I opened my door slowly and peered into the hallway. The bathroom door was open, and her bedroom door was closed.

In bare feet I crossed the hall and knocked softly on her door. I heard a very low, strangled, "Yes?"

"You can have the shower first. I'll just stay in my room until I hear you go downstairs."

Silence. I pressed my ear to the door. Did she say something, and I just didn't hear her? "Don't use all the hot water," I teased.

All I got back was another low, strangled word. "Okay."

With a deep sigh, I headed back to my room. *Maybe I* had *better invest in a hearing aid,* I thought glumly.

I quickly discovered it was a lot more awkward than I'd imagined possible to sit across the breakfast table from a stranger who I had seen in her skivvies.

I'd seen girls in bikinis before, some bikinis that revealed more than Robin's underwear had. But it wasn't the same. Bras and panties, by their very nature, hinted at intimacy.

Robin wouldn't even look at me. She talked quietly—naturally, very quietly—to my mum. She completely ignored me.

So I'd seen her in her underwear. So what! So what? She was cute in her underwear. Very cute. Soft curves. Flat stomach. She even had tan lines. That's what.

I could see the red flush that was still on her face.

At least she was dressed normally today in jeans, a jumper, and trainers. An image of what she was wearing beneath all that clothing flashed through my mind. I felt the heat warm my face. I wished that my dad were sitting at the table so I'd at least have someone to talk to. But my dad always slept in on Sunday morning. Which I had really wanted to do as well.

I pushed that thought aside before my irritation with this whole situation got out of hand. The tension at the table was thick enough to cut with a butter knife. My whole last day before school started was ruined because I had to take her to the Tower, and she was treating me like I had the plague. I needed to get out of here, cool down, and decide what to do.

"Mum, I'm done. I'll be waiting by the front

door for Robin," I said, addressing the table at large.

My mum glanced over her shoulder as though only just noticing I was there.

"Certainly, dear," she said quickly before turning her attention back to Robin.

Great! Now not only could I not walk into my own hallway in my underwear, I was being ignored by my mum.

I strode to the entryway, leaned against the front door, and crossed my arms over my chest. So far, hosting a YA student was nothing like I expected it to be. Was I going to have to live the whole year walking on eggshells just because I'd stepped out of my room without thinking, out of habit? Not likely.

I'd apologize to Robin. A very straightforward apology. Simple and clean. It would put the horrid shower incident—as I was beginning to think of it—behind us. We could then move forward. Knowing how formal Robin tended to be, I decided that I needed to be equally formal in order to gain her attention.

My dear Miss Carter, my humblest apologies if I offended your sensibilities this morning when I unwittingly stepped into the hallway in my just-crawled-out-of-bed attire as I had every morning for as long as I can remember.

Right. That one was fairly sickening. She would no doubt love it.

She came into the foyer. I opened the front door and watched her trudge outside, her head bent. Her face was set in an expressionless mask. I wondered briefly if I should just skip the apology. Forget this morning ever happened.

No, no, it was best to face things head-on.

I followed her out and waited until I'd closed the door firmly behind us. I had to hurry to catch up to her, and her apparent embarrassment was making me feel a tad awkward. "Er, sorry 'bout before," I offered. So much for my formal apology.

She plastered a frozen smile onto her face but kept marching forward like a determined soldier. "It's okay. Let's pretend it never happened."

I almost asked her to repeat what she'd said, but I thought I'd caught the gist of most of it.

"It could have been worse. We might have been wearing nothing at all," I teased, trying to chip something off the iceberg building between us.

She jerked her head around and glared at me.

I felt my face turn red. "Best to forget about it," I agreed as I fell into step beside her and directed her toward the tube.

Fantastic. She didn't have a sense of humor. She couldn't speak above a whisper. And she'd seen me in my underwear.

I had a whole blasted year with her to look forward to. I could barely contain my excitement at the prospect.

Five

Robin

THE SUBWAY! THE tube was the subway.

  I sat on the seat beside Kit as the train flew between stations. I sneaked a peek at him as he stared at the advertisements plastered on the side across from us. Could this morning get any worse? I was beyond mortified.

  At least my natural shriek had been appropriate. It hadn't contained an ounce of twang. Just pure one hundred percent humiliation.

  How could I have walked into the hall wearing nothing but my underwear and a blush? Only one explanation made sense. Between the jet lag and waking up forgetting where I was, I had walked out of my room thinking I was at home!

  I have got to stay alert and keep my guard up, I reminded myself.

I couldn't let Kit distract me. And he had certainly done that in the hallway, standing there in nothing but his briefs. I wouldn't have freaked out if he'd been standing in sand, on a beach. In that situation I would have even admired his body.

Okay, I had admired it in the hallway as well. But that was beside the point. He had remained calm, while I had totally freaked out. He'd even had the presence of mind to come and tell me I could shower first while I'd been trying to decide how to take a bath using only the water that was in the pitcher on the bedside table.

And he seemed to have a sense of humor. It would have been worse if we'd been wearing nothing at all.

Without looking at me, he murmured, "Sorry my dad put you through the grand inquisition last night."

I shifted on the seat. "He was just being curious."

He grimaced. "Only because curiosity is his job. He's a solicitor."

"Ah, a telemarketer," I commented softly with a nod.

He leaned toward me, his brow creased. "Pardon?"

Oh gosh. Now I didn't know if he hadn't heard me or he didn't know what a telemarketer was. Trying to hide my accent was almost more trouble than it was worth. He was so cute and seemed really nice. I was almost tempted to be myself.

But then what would he think? That he had

52

Dr. Jekyll and Miz Hyde living in his house for a year?

Nope, I'd set my path, and now I had to follow it. Besides, who knew what he'd tell kids at school?

I decided to speak a little louder and give a little more explanation, so I covered all my bases. I cleared my throat. "A telemarketer. An individual who solicits people on the telephone and attempts to convince them to purchase items such as neon headbands."

He gave me his shy grin. "That's what I thought you meant. I think in the States that you call my dad's profession being a lawyer."

I felt the heat flush my cheeks. I was riding the tube with a bloke whose dad was a solicitor. I absolutely wanted to scream. It was like talking in a foreign language—only worse because I knew the words. I just didn't always know what they meant.

"You never did tell my dad what your dad does," he said over the din of rumbling tracks.

No, I hadn't. If Kit was asking me a question, I didn't hear the question mark. When would we get to our stop?

"What does he do?" Kit asked.

Question mark. Dadgum it. It was there loud and clear, and I couldn't very well ignore it.

"He's into agriculture," I said evasively. That wasn't a lie, although my dad would have said it was pretentious. "Honey, I'm just a farmer," he always said, like it was no big deal that he worked seventy hours a week for less than minimum wage so people would find food in the produce section of their grocery stores.

I felt the train begin to slow. *Please be our stop. Please be our stop.*

Kit stood. "Here's our stop."

I let out a great gust of air and got to my feet as the train halted. We stepped onto the platform.

"It's just a bit of a walk," he said, shoving his hands into his jeans pockets.

When we strolled out of the station, I knew how the country mouse felt when she went to the city. I wanted to grab Kit's arm and point at the buildings and ask him what they were. Instead I balled my hands into tight fists and shoved them into the pockets of my jeans. I knew my jaw had dropped to my knees and my eyes were as big and circular as a harvest moon, but I couldn't help it.

"Right, here we are," Kit said, and I felt like I'd been thrown back in time.

I had been expecting a solitary tower like the one Rapunzel sat in. I wasn't expecting this huge stone complex with turrets and towers.

I saw Dana and Carrie at the entrance. My pulse picked up its tempo. What a relief! Everything didn't seem so overwhelming now. I almost shouted to them but caught myself just in time. As long as Kit was beside me, I had to be sophisticated and very low-key. Ugh! Why couldn't he have had some plans for today?

Carrie and Dana greeted me with wide grins. I offered them a small smile. Ladylike and sophisticated.

"I'm so pleased you could make it," I said softly.

Dana rolled her eyes, and Carrie gave me a slap on the back that nearly sent me staggering forward.

"We are too," Carrie said loudly. Her drawl, not quite as pronounced as mine, echoed around us. I never thought I'd welcome the sound of a Texas twang.

"We went to Covent Garden last night," Dana told me. "We sure missed you."

"I would have liked to have shared the experience with you," I said. "But I needed to get accustomed to my new home."

"And your new brother," Carrie announced with teasing laced in her voice.

Kit cleared his throat and looked at me, his eyes twinkling. "We both had some things to get accustomed to."

I knew he was thinking of our close encounter in the hallway on our way to the shower. How could he joke about it?

"Today is my parents' treat," he said. "I'm going to pop over and get the tickets."

As soon as he was out of earshot, Carrie and Dana closed ranks around me.

"Okay. Give us the entire scoop," Carrie demanded.

"You seemed to have survived your first night living with a guy," Dana mused.

"Barely," I declared. I felt my body blush from the top of my head to the tips of my toes. "I had a close encounter of the most embarrassing kind! This morning I, like, forgot that I wasn't at home. You know that I don't wake up quickly. So I headed for the shower wearing only my bra and panties. I staggered into the hallway—and there he was, on his way to the shower, wearing the same thing!"

"He wears a bra?" Dana inquired, clearly startled.

"No, goofus," I said, feeling like I was completely losing my ability to communicate. "He was only wearing his briefs! I was totally mortified. It was the single most humiliating experience of my entire existence."

"Oh my gosh." Carrie sighed dreamily. "What did he look like? I want details."

"Like any normal guy wearing a bathing suit— only it was his underwear," I explained.

"I've seen my brothers in their underwear. It's no big deal," Carrie assured me.

"No big deal? I shrieked at the top of my lungs and hightailed it back to my room. I wanted to die," I muttered dejectedly.

"Your reaction was normal," Dana assured me.

"Yeah, for someone from bump-in-the-road Mustang, Texas. I should have remained calm and poised and just turned around and walked back into my room as though I saw guys in their briefs all the time," I murmured.

Dana shook her head. "That was probably the first time he actually saw you as yourself."

"That's what I'm afraid of," I confided. "I almost ruined my cover."

"Oh, Robin, you need to be yourself," Dana insisted.

"Oh yeah, right. Jason was from big-city Dallas, and he thought I was a backwoods hillbilly farm girl. What do you think Kit would think of the real me? The dare-me-to-do-anything Robin Carter who has the worst twang, worst way of speaking, and most embarrassing loud, brash personality?"

"I think he'd like you as much as we do," Dana told me.

I had a lot more I wanted to say, but Kit returned with our tickets.

"Thank you," I said as I took my ticket from him. "I appreciate your parents' thoughtfulness."

"Right," Kit said in a clipped British accent.

"Let's head for the crown jewels," Carrie suggested. She slipped her arm through Kit's. "Do you think they'll let me try them on?"

Kit's laughter echoed around me as Carrie led him toward the entrance. I felt an unexpected pang of jealousy. Carrie was always comfortable with guys, but then, guys liked her.

Following them, Dana leaned toward me and whispered, "You sound completely unfriendly and unfun talking in that low, formal voice without your accent."

I stared at her, unable to believe that Dana still didn't get it.

"That's how I'm trying to sound."

"Can y'all believe these crowns?" Carrie asked. "I've never seen so many different jewels. And they're huge! Huge!"

I couldn't believe it either. The gold, the diamonds, the sapphires, the emeralds, the silver. Like Carrie, I was completely in awe. I turned to the guard standing nearby. "Are these jewels real?"

He wrinkled his nose as if he smelled something foul and looked down at me. "Yes, miss. After all, this is not Disney World."

I wanted to die of mortification. I heard snickers from the tour group behind me. Would I never learn what to say and not to say in front of people?

I glared over my shoulder at Carrie and Dana and said with my eyes, "See, I *need* help!"

Carrie and Dana just rolled their eyes toward the snobbish guard. But then, they weren't the ones who had experienced the humiliation of being told in front of a crowd of students near the guy they liked that they were uncouth and obnoxious.

"This isn't Disney World?" Kit whispered to me. "One look at the guard's Mickey Mouse–like ears, and I thought that's where we were!"

I couldn't help myself. I burst out laughing. The guard glared at me, but he had lost his power over me because of Kit's comment.

I wanted to sling my arms around Kit's neck and thank him for coming to my rescue. But I couldn't do that. I had to remain demure, even though I'd slipped for a moment there.

As the group continued the tour, I avoided standing close to Kit. He was too cute, too English, too intimidating, too male, and too un-expectedly nice and funny. *I can't like him,* I warned myself. *I absolutely cannot! He would be horrified by the real me. I would never be able to talk above a whisper if I liked him. I'd never be able to be myself. Don't like him!*

That order was a lot easier to give than to obey. But obey it I would or risk humiliation far worse than I had suffered that morning.

My feet were aching by the end of the afternoon, and my enthusiasm was waning. How could anything that housed something as beautiful as the crown jewels also hold Traitor's Gate and the Bloody Tower? I hated hearing about the young princes who had probably been murdered. Richard of Gloucester had taken them to the tower, and

59

they'd never been seen again. He was later crowned king.

As though sensing that we were saddened by the Tower and its woe, Kit took us to see the ravens next. They were only black birds, but I thought they looked somewhat majestic.

"Legend has it that if the ravens ever leave the Tower, Britain will fall," Kit explained.

I wished I didn't enjoy the musical cadence of his voice so much.

"And they never fly away?" Dana asked. "That's amazing."

Kit cleared his throat and shifted from one foot to the other, looking extremely uncomfortable.

Carrie plopped her hands onto her hips. "All right, Kit, out with it. What aren't you telling us?"

He grimaced. "They clip their wings so they can't fly."

My stomach rolled. I loved animals. Had rescued fallen birds and nursed barn owls back to health.

"Sorry," Kit said, and I knew he meant it. For some reason, I wished that he hadn't meant it.

"Well, on that cheerful note," Carrie said, "we're gonna have to go."

"So soon?" I asked. The afternoon had passed so quickly. When Kit wasn't standing nearby, I had been able to be myself, laughing, joking, groaning. How would I survive this year without my two best friends?

"We're supposed to meet Miss Lawrence at the entrance at five," Dana explained.

"Let's say good-bye here," Carrie suggested. "Then when Dana and I walk away, it won't seem like we're really leaving."

I felt the tears sting my eyes. "It's gonna feel like you're leaving no matter what we do."

I slung my arms around my closest friends, and tears slid along my cheeks. I wasn't only saying good-bye to them; I was saying good-bye to myself. It was only around them that I could ever be the true Robin.

"Y'all had better e-mail me every day or else," I ordered.

"You'd better e-mail us," Carrie told me.

"I will as soon as I get home. . . . Well, not home." I released choked laughter. "Not my real home. My home here. You know what I mean. I'm babbling."

"You're babbling," Dana repeated.

"Watch out for those guys in Paris," I warned Dana.

Dana wiggled her eyebrows. "I plan to watch them very closely."

I laughed again while the tears continued to fall. I knew Dana wanted to fall in love in Paris.

"Carrie—," I began.

"I know, I know, watch out for the Italians." She smiled brightly and looked past me. "Kit, you take care of our friend."

"I will," he said quietly.

My heart slammed against my ribs. I'd forgotten he was nearby. Gosh, he'd seen and heard everything. I wiped the tears from my face and tried to recompose myself. I threw back my shoulders and lifted my chin.

"Have an amazing year abroad," I said in a low, accent-free voice.

Dana leaned close and whispered with a cunning look in her eyes, "Too late."

My heart sank. I was afraid that might be the case.

I watched Dana and Carrie loop their arms around each other's waists and head for the entrance. Oh, it hurt. I wanted to call after them, but I had to try to repair any damage I might have done while saying good-bye.

As it was, Kit probably thought he was living with a total freak!

Six

Robin

SITTING ON THE window seat, hugging my bent knees against my chest, I stared out my bedroom window while the lights of London glowed against the black sky. Saying good-bye to my friends had been so hard. Riding home on the tube with Kit in silence had been so hard. Eating dinner with the Marlins tonight had been so hard. And now being alone in my room was so hard!

I wished I could call my friends, but I couldn't. I hadn't really considered all that was involved in the YA program when I'd accepted Dana and Carrie's dare to join them in the program. Until this moment I hadn't truly realized that I was on my own here, so far from home, from anything familiar. Where were my pigs when I needed them? I knew my dad was feeding them, but I still worried about them. Did they miss me?

Someone knocked on the door. My stomach knotted tightly. Keeping up this facade of a demure, sophisticated Robin was suddenly too much. Tears started to sting the backs of my eyes.

I cleared my throat. Irritating tears were hovering there too.

"Come in," I croaked, hardly sounding sophisticated. I tried to blink back the tears, but they were stubborn and refused to go away. Instead they seemed to be inviting all their friends to a party. *Join us, and the party can spill out of her eyes and onto her cheeks.*

Kit walked into the room. I'd really been hoping for Mrs. Marlin. She would understand the tears. But a guy? No way.

I stared down at the hardwood floor so he wouldn't see the sign of my weakness. His feet came into view. Well, not his feet, exactly. The socks covering his feet. I'd never seen a guy without shoes. But then, I'd never seen a guy without clothes either. It looked like this year I was going to experience a lot of firsts—and not all of them pleasant.

"I'm creating a schedule so we won't be caught again in something like what happened this morning," he explained.

A corner of my mouth fought to lift into a smile. He'd said schedule wrong. *Shedule* was what it sounded like instead of *skedule*. The English. Didn't they know anything?

"Did you want the bathroom first or second in the morning?" he asked.

"I'll take the bathroom first," I whispered.

I felt him studying me. I pressed my knees hard against my chest, wanting to curl into a ball of misery. Why wouldn't he leave so I could let the tears fall?

"Are you from a different part of Texas than your friends?" Kit asked.

Huh? What was he talking about? I wondered.

Not daring to look at him, I watched his toes wiggle up and down in his socks.

"I was just curious because you don't sound like they do," he explained.

Disappointment reeled through me. I slid my eyes closed. So much for trying to disguise my voice. He'd seen right through me.

"I mean, they actually talk like cowboys in old Western movies," he went on, "but your voice has hardly any trace of accent."

My eyes flew open. He hadn't noticed my accent. I was pulling it off! I was really pulling it off. Now to keep up the illusion, all I had to do was reverse the truth.

"They're, um, from a farm, and I'm, um, from town," I murmured in my low, accent-free voice. It was almost becoming second nature to talk like this. Before long, I wouldn't have to think about it.

I would talk this way naturally. "We townspeople have less of an accent."

"I like their accents," he told me.

"You do?" I blurted out in my deep Texas twang. I slapped my hand over my mouth and glared out the window. So much for second nature. Who could have missed that loud, brash question?

He dropped down on the window seat beside me. I drew myself more tightly into a ball. What a lame thing to do! Two words had totally blown two days' worth of effort.

"Why are you hiding your real way of speaking?" he inquired, clearly confused.

Into my silence he added, "I find your accent charming, especially when you said 'y'all' as you were threatening your friends, telling them they'd better e-mail every day or else."

I scoffed and continued glaring out the window.

"Do you plan to whisper for a whole year?" he asked.

Being mute would have been better. I was afraid I was going to break down into heart-wrenching sobs. As much as I hated to admit it, Kit was so totally right. Today had been a nightmare, talking normal around my friends, talking low whenever he came near. Now Dana and Carrie were gone, and I'd never be able to talk normal again—at least not for a year anyway.

Overwhelmed by that realization, I jerked my gaze to his and blurted out exactly what I was feeling, even if it wasn't the answer to the question he'd posed. "I'm as lonely as the last star before sunrise."

He smiled tenderly, and I felt more tears surface. I dropped my gaze quickly before he caught sight of them.

"Of course you're lonely," he said gently. "You're really far from home and your friends. But you'll be fine. You've got me for a brother, after all."

I glanced up at him, unable to believe how nice he was. I swiped the tears from my eyes. "Some people don't like small-town Texas accents," I explained, thinking of Jason's comment that I sounded like I was putting on the slow drawl.

"Then they're idiots," he told me. "Your accent is charming."

He was the one with the charming accent. I sniffed. "It's embarrassing."

"It shouldn't be. It's part of who you are," he explained.

I didn't figure now was the time to tell him that my accent wasn't the only thing I'd been hiding. I was hiding my entire personality. Texas Robin would have been pacing by now. But I had my arms wrapped around my legs so tightly that I was in danger of cutting off my circulation.

I gave him a shaky smile and a promise. "I won't whisper anymore."

He released a deep breath. "Am I ever glad to

hear that! I thought I might go hoarse saying, 'Sorry?' all the time."

I released a small, self-conscious giggle.

"You do realize that I was afraid I was going deaf, don't you?" he asked.

He was making me feel completely silly for ever trying to hide my voice, but he was doing it in a way that didn't make me feel . . . as ungainly as a cow. He wasn't ridiculing me for trying to hide my accent, but he'd managed to coax me into revealing it, and I figured he might not laugh if I confessed something else.

"About school tomorrow . . . I'm as nervous as a long-tailed cat in a room full of rocking chairs," I confided.

"Don't be. You're going to be a huge hit." He leaned close as if to impart a secret. "As long as you don't whisper," he whispered so low that *I* almost said "pardon!"

So much for not liking him. I was falling harder for Kit than I'd ever fallen for anyone, even snot Jason.

He stood and stretched. "Well, I'd best be off to bed. Just give a brisk knock on my door in the morning when you're done with the bathroom."

I watched him stroll casually across the room. He stopped at my door and glanced over his shoulder. He smiled warmly. "Good night, sis."

Sis? Huh? He thinks of me as a sister?

Ugh. That figures.

But there was totally no way I could possibly think of him as a brother.

Seven

Robin

NERVOUS WRECK. THAT was an apt description for how I felt sitting at the breakfast table the next morning. My first day of English school! This was ten times worse than the first day of school at Mustang. At least there I had Carrie and Dana for moral support.

Even though I had slathered butter on my English muffin, it felt like sawdust in my mouth. And I absolutely could not dip my spoon into the boiled egg that was sitting upright in a tiny cup—its top lobbed off. The yolk was still shimmering! I liked to make sure my eggs were dead before I ate them, and this one looked like it had only recently been plucked from the henhouse.

I gulped some milk and glanced at the clock on the wall. If a watched pot never boiled, maybe the hands on a clock wouldn't move if they were watched.

I really needed more time to adjust before going to school in London. Just a little more time. Like . . . a year, maybe.

"Don't be so nervous," Kit ordered.

It had been so quiet at the table that it was like his voice came out of nowhere. My body jerked, each limb working on its own. I thought of that cat in the cartoons that shrieks and ends up hanging upside down with its claws digging into the ceiling. That could have easily been me at that moment.

How could he sound so calm?

"You'll probably find that my school is a lot like your own," he added.

Uh-huh, I thought. *Right. So far everything has been exactly like Mustang, Texas. Not!*

My stomach felt like it was a tangle of string creating Jacob's ladder by the time Kit told me that we needed to leave. I grabbed my backpack off a side table where I'd set it earlier.

"You'll probably want to take your mac," he said as we walked toward the door.

"Oh, great!" I exclaimed before hurrying up the stairs. Taking computers to school was definitely not the way it was done in Mustang. Cool! I'd be able to take notes in class—notes I could actually read later. I dashed into my room, unplugged my computer from the socket and the phone jack, and quickly packed it into its small case.

I rushed back down the stairs. Kit was waiting by the door. "Got it!" I cried, holding up my laptop.

He furrowed his brow. "Your mac?"

I nodded.

A corner of his mouth lifted as if he was on the verge of finally understanding the punch line to some joke. "Your mackintosh?" he asked.

I held my computer higher. "My Macintosh!"

He lifted his coat off his arm. "Raincoat."

I felt like a total idiot. So much for being able to read my notes. I made another quick dash upstairs to put away my computer and grab my raincoat.

Everything's called something else in England, I realized glumly. What if I made a total fool of myself in school? That possibility was looming before me as a definite reality.

I couldn't even enjoy the walk to school. I was too busy studying my feet, trying to make sure that they kept moving forward—instead of going off in the direction that they wanted, which was back.

"Sorry?" Kit inquired beside me.

I jerked my gaze up to his. He wore this incredible heart-stopping smile, and his eyes held this teasing glint in them.

"I thought you said something," he explained.

I shook my head, baffled. "No."

"Ah, that's right. I forgot. From now on, you're going to talk loudly enough for people to hear you, right?" he teased.

It felt good to laugh. "Right," I agreed, smiling brightly.

He slipped his arm around me and gave my shoulder a quick squeeze. "You're going to do just fine," he assured me.

He dropped his arm to his side, and my lungs started drawing in air again. I told myself that it had been a . . . brotherly hug. No big deal. Just because his touch made my heartbeat double . . .

We reached the school, and I had to admit that Kit had been right. From the outside, it wasn't that much different from Mustang High. Brick building. Windows. Doors. Concrete walks.

The difference was the people. I didn't know anybody!

My nervous level shot up like the mercury in a thermometer that was placed in boiling water.

"Hey, Kit!" a guy yelled, and hurried over.

"Hey, Peter," Kit greeted him.

"New love?" Peter inquired.

Kit laughed lightly and put his hand on the small of my back, a comforting gesture, I told myself, because he knew I was nervous. Plus he was probably trying to quiet the thudding of my heart.

"Robin is our Year Abroad student," Kit explained.

Peter wrinkled his entire face as if it helped him think. He had spiked blond hair, and when he wasn't talking, he could easily pass for a guy from Mustang High.

"Thought our YAS was a guy," he mused.

"Right, but in my excitement over being selected to host the YAS, I didn't read the information packet closely enough. Robin's our girl," Kit said.

I liked the thought of being someone's girl. Especially since I'd never been anyone's girl. It gave me a warm, snuggly feeling.

Peter grinned broadly. "So what do you think so far?"

The moment of truth had come. Kit's hand moved to my shoulder, and I knew I could do this. All I had to do was answer as demurely as possible, toning down my accent while still being audible. "It's different over here."

Kit squeezed my shoulder, and I knew I'd pulled it off.

"In what ways?" Peter asked.

I was spared answering when a girl with long, black hair that had one purple streak down the center approached.

"Is she the YAS?" the girl queried.

Kit's hand moved back to my waist as he introduced me to Zoe. It was so reassuring to have the pressure of Kit's hand on my waist, my back, my shoulder. I felt like I wasn't alone here.

Zoe was bouncing questions off me, one right after the other, like she was conducting an interview, only she never let me answer. Even when more people circled us and she was eased aside, I could still hear her asking questions.

Kit was making introductions left and right, and the questions were coming fast and furious. I knew students from other countries were popular at Mustang High, but I'd always figured it was the novelty of something different in a town that should have been named Boredom. I hadn't expected sophisticated Londoners to take more than a passing interest in me.

I was actually beginning to feel like I was smothering with all the attention.

"All right, all right," Kit finally cut in. "You all have a year to ask your questions. Right now, I've got to get Robin to the main office."

He put his hand on my back and propelled me forward through the crowd.

"Welcome, Robin!"

"Save me a place at lunch, Rob!"

"See you in class, Robin!"

"We're glad you're here!"

I wanted to laugh with complete and absolute joy. They liked me. They actually seemed to like the new me that I was striving to become. I had held my accent at bay.

"Shouldn't you call back that it was nice meeting *y'all?*" Kit asked once we'd moved beyond the maddening crowd.

I shook my head. "I'm really trying to tone down my accent."

"Why?" he asked, sounding completely baffled.

"Because it's so utterly country."

He opened his mouth to say something, but before he could speak, a girl stepped out from behind a pillar, swept in front of him, and planted a major doozy of a kiss smack-dab on his lips. Sorta like she owned those lips of his.

Shock waves rippled through me as I watched him fold his arms around her.

He drew back and bestowed upon her a hundred-megawatt smile. "I didn't realize how much I'd missed you."

"It was the most miserable summer of my life, and all because you weren't there." She spoke in a soft, cultured voice.

I thought I was going to be ill. Had I actually thought that Kit could be more than a brother? Of course a guy as cute as he was had a girlfriend. What was I thinking?

With one arm still wrapped possessively around the girl—who happened to be more beautiful than any girl should be—Kit turned toward me. With a cute laugh, he introduced me. "Brooke, this is my sister, Robin."

Brooke gave me an icy glare and snapped, "I thought the exchange student was a guy."

Kit laughed a little self-consciously and rubbed

the side of his nose. "Actually, so did I. It's been quite an adjustment."

That was an understatement.

"Listen, I've got to get Robin to the main office, so I'll catch up with you later." Kit brushed a quick kiss over her upturned cheek.

She smiled, and I thought of a witch out of a Disney movie.

She flicked her flowing blond hair over her shoulder. "I'll just tag along."

And she did, wedging herself between Kit and me. The absence of his nearness caused my nerves to go on full-scale alert. I suddenly felt incredibly alone even though this brazen blond babe was walking beside me.

"So, have you a boyfriend back in the States?" she inquired.

At that moment I considered fudging the truth and telling her that I did have, but we'd decided to date other people during our year apart, but I was already being so unfaithful to my true self that I decided I should opt for the truth. "No, no boyfriend."

"Someone you like?" she prodded.

I couldn't figure out where she was going with this. There seemed to be a little more to her tone than "inquiring minds want to know."

"There's a lot of people that I like," I pointed out.

"I was thinking of someone specific, someone you fancy, someone you're pining after, who you're hoping will miss you so much while you're away that he'll fall at your feet when you return," she said.

She'd hit a little too close to home with that scenario. "No, no one."

"Mmmm. Well, maybe that'll change here. The YAS is usually an instant smash. Appearance, personality, being hip really don't come into the play because the YAS is so absolutely novel," she purred.

I had the feeling that I'd just been insulted.

"Here's the main office," Kit said as we rounded a corner.

Through the wide, double-glass doors I could see a long counter and two women standing behind it. Just like the office at Mustang High.

"Did you want me to go with you?" Kit asked.

"No, I'll be just fine," I assured him, smiling brightly.

I turned and headed for the doors. The truth was, I desperately wanted to get away from Brooke.

Her cold shoulder was giving me frostbite.

Eight

Robin

I WAS INCREDIBLY relieved to see Kit when I walked into my creative-writing class. One friendly face!

He smiled at me and tipped his head toward the empty desk beside him. I returned his smile. I didn't want to be anywhere else.

As I took a step forward, someone brushed by me. I watched in stunned silence as Brooke gracefully slid into the chair that I had planned to drop into. I halfway expected Kit to explain to her that seat was taken.

He lowered his head as she whispered something to him. He gave her a soft smile. Then he looked at me and pointed to the desk behind him.

I shook my head and sat at a desk in the front. No way did I want to be in a position to watch them making goo-goo eyes at each other during class.

All morning my classes had distracted me, so that I'd almost forgotten how surprised and surprisingly hurt I'd been to see another girl kiss Kit. But that hurt hit sharply now like a stab to my heart. I glanced over my shoulder. Brooke gave me a cold look. I wondered how she washed her face. Water must freeze the moment it touched her skin.

The teacher rapped her ruler on the desk to gain attention. I shifted in my seat. *Mrs. Lambourne* was written in bold, purple script across the white dry-erase board.

"I expect this term to be an amazing experience for all of you. We are fortunate enough to have our Year Abroad student in this class." She pierced me with her gaze and raised her hands, palms up, like she was a magician levitating a prone body. "Stand up, please."

Inwardly I groaned. I'd gone through this ritual in every class so far. I stood. I still hadn't figured out where I was supposed to look. Should I focus on the teacher? Should I sweep my gaze around the room? Maybe I should just stare at the floor or ponder the pattern on the ceiling.

"Robin Carter has traveled all the way from Mustang, Texas, to be with us this year," Mrs. Lambourne said, as if she were personally responsible for my being here. "Turn around so everyone can get a good look at you."

Now I knew how criminals in a police lineup felt. I could sense everyone gawking at me and imagined them pointing fingers. "That's her! She's the one! She did it! Off with her head!"

I turned, and my eyes immediately fell on Kit. He winked and gave me a thumbs-up signal. Such a little thing, but it really restored my confidence.

Mrs. Lambourne gave me permission to sit, and it was only when I sat that I realized I was trembling. I'd had no idea that being popular could be so nerve-racking.

Mrs. Lambourne went into a spiel on the dynamics of creativity. I furiously took notes only because it distracted me from the fact that Kit sat at the back of the room with Brooke. I wondered briefly why he hadn't mentioned her, but when I thought about it, I realized we hadn't really talked, hadn't really gotten a chance to know each other. My low talking had managed to put a wall between us, and I regretted that I'd taken that approach in the beginning.

"Your first assignment," Mrs. Lambourne announced in a way that reminded me of drumrolls, "will be an oral presentation to be delivered next Monday."

My heart very nearly stopped beating, and I found myself staring at her. Oral? This class was creative *writing!* I had specifically avoided signing up for any classes that even hinted they might require someone to speak.

"The topic I selected will allow you to share yourself with your fellow classmates—'My Goal for This Semester,' whether it be to get better marks, learn to play the guitar, sleep more, what have you."

This assignment was the worst I'd ever been given. My goal was to go from hillbilly farm girl with the heaviest southern drawl to sophisticated, reserved Princess Di type. There was no way that I could admit that openly to my fellow classmates! Maybe I could talk about hoping to learn about English culture or finding my way around the roundabouts or something.

But how was I gonna get through an oral presentation and hide my accent and my usual way of talking? I could handle it a few words at a time, but we were talking paragraphs here, possibly pages!

As soon as the dismissal bell rang, I approached Mrs. Lambourne. She smiled brightly and swept her fist through the air in a silent, jolly-good-show movement.

"I'm so pleased you're in my class," she said enthusiastically.

"I thought this was a writing class," I admitted.

"Of course it is. First you write the essay, and then you present it orally," she explained.

"I don't mean to be obtuse, but wouldn't it be better just to let everyone read our essays? You know? Writers write so people can read their words," I pointed out, hoping she'd see the correlation.

She shook her head. "It's necessary to expose the essence of yourself to the class. The more vulnerable you become, the more deeply you will write." She patted my shoulder. "I look so forward to hearing your presentation. I shall no doubt let you go first."

Was that supposed to make me look forward to Black Monday, as I'd already dubbed that dreaded day? I walked out of the room, dragging my feet and my expectations. I had seven days to get rid of the accent. A crash course was in order.

Popular was not a word that I usually associated with myself. So it was a little unnerving at lunch to find myself surrounded by people I didn't know—who were incredibly anxious to know me.

My plan had been to casually eavesdrop on a table of English girls here and a table of English girls there. But that was not to be.

The table I sat at seated six, and five girls quickly joined me. They were an excitable group.

"Your jumper is smashing," Zoe said. I remembered meeting her that morning.

I had no idea what a jumper was, so I simply smiled and faked it. "Thanks. So is yours."

Her eyes grew wide, and she barked out her laughter. "I'm not wearing one."

Did I feel foolish! I offered her a sheepish grin. "Sorry."

The girl sitting next to me, Beth, pulled on the sleeve of my pullover sweater. "Jumper."

I grimaced. "Ah, sweater."

"Why does it have a horse embroidered on the shoulder?" Zoe asked.

I touched the emblem. I'd worn the pullover so I wouldn't miss my old school so much. "It's a mustang. My school's mascot." My explanation probably made no sense to them, but they all smiled brightly and nodded. I figured we were all faking it. Maybe we weren't so different after all.

I really wanted them to talk more so I could learn to imitate their speech. I needed a question that required a detailed explanation. "What did everyone do over the school break?"

"I went on holiday to the seaside," one girl said.

"Tamara always goes on holiday to the seaside," Zoe explained. "She likes to see the fellows in their bathing trunks."

"You'd better believe it," Tamara said.

"My dad took me up to Scotland in his lorry," a girl named Lizzie told me. "I enjoyed seeing the countryside." She grinned and glanced mischievously around the table. "But I'd rather see the lads at the seaside."

I had no idea what a lorry was. How was I supposed to emulate these girls with their sophisticated, elegant ways when I couldn't understand half their words? I was beginning to think I needed a British-American dictionary. I was never gonna make it here!

Zoe tapped my shoulder with a perfectly manicured finger. I bet she'd never tossed manure onto her dad's fields to ensure that they had a good crop come fall.

"What are the lads like in Texas?" she asked.

What I had wanted to avoid was suddenly dropped in my lap. A question directed at me. "Not that much different than the guys here."

Zoe leaned forward on her elbows, zeal in her gaze. "Oh, come on. Give us a bit more than that. How do they kiss?"

"Yes, how do they kiss?" a very cultured voice asked behind me.

I looked over my shoulder, and there stood Brooke, her eyebrows raised. The bloodred lipstick on one corner of her mouth was slightly smudged, and I wondered if she'd been kissing Kit again. Until I'd seen her in a lip lock with him, I hadn't realized how much of a lifeline Kit had become since our talk last night. Or how much I liked him.

He suddenly appeared beside Brooke and grinned. "How's it going?"

I offered him a smile of bravado. "Interesting."

"I'll just bet. You'll have to tell me all about it when we get home. You gonna eat your biscuit?" he asked.

I glanced at my plate. I didn't have a biscuit. I

didn't even have a roll or a slice of bread. But I knew he wouldn't deliberately try to embarrass me, so something on my plate was a biscuit. I looked back at him and shook my head. He snatched the cookie off my plate. "Got to get to class."

I watched him walk off with Brooke. I was alone in a strange country, and he had reached out a friendly hand when I most needed one. But it wasn't like I could ever hope to win his heart.

A proper, reserved English guy like Kit going for a girl who had to hide her personality? Ha. He had thought it was charming that I had felt the need to hide my cute li'l accent. What would he think if he knew I'd been voted Queen of the Dare and Most Talkative every year in school?

Well, I wouldn't win those awards next year, I vowed as I stood, slung my backpack over my shoulder, and picked up my tray. Next year I'd win Most Changed for the Better!

Nine

Robin

I HAD HOPED that the second day of school would be easier than the first. But no such luck. If anything, it was harder. The rumor had circulated. I was the YAS.

I actually had a fan club. Well, it wasn't the Robin Carter fan club, exactly. It was the YAS fan club, and I was by default the official mascot. Before class started, after class started, in the hallways, in the cafeteria, in the atrium—girls stopped to ask me questions.

I was afraid that my conversion to sophisticated Robin was going to be limited to sentences that ended in a question mark. It was hard to grab the right inflection on normal sentences when all I heard were questions. The upside was that most of the questions could be answered with one word.

Fortunately, guys were not enamored of my special YAS status. Most looked at me as if I were a five-legged calf, and they couldn't quite decide if that fifth leg was interesting or just plain weird.

That was fine with me for the time being. Until I had nurtured my changed image and felt comfortable with it, I really didn't want any guys talking to me.

Well, that wasn't exactly true. I craved Kit talking to me the way I craved chocolate. It was a fact of my life that I needed chocolate to survive.

And I was beginning to realize that I needed Kit too.

Strolling home with him yesterday had been the best part of the day. His reassurance that I was a hit had gone a long way toward giving me the courage to walk through the school doors today.

Yesterday I had also learned that afternoon tea was a British ritual. Sitting at the table, drinking tea, and eating chocolate digestive biscuits with Kit and his mom had been . . . well, perfect. I'd felt like such a lady with the dainty teacup and the china saucer.

I thought classes today would never come to an end. When the final bell rang, I released a grateful sigh. I had somehow, through no fault of my own, managed to survive without disclosing my deep, dark twang. A true miracle, considering all the questions I had answered.

I sauntered into the hallway, almost feeling invincible. I noticed a banner slung across the top of the doors.

Get Acquainted Social, Monday, September 11, 7 P.M.

Black Monday. After giving my oral presentation, unless I could tame this wild accent, I didn't figure I'd be welcomed at any social. The thought left me rather glum.

But I cheered up considerably when I caught up with Kit at the atrium. My heart did a little tap dance when he smiled at me.

"How was your day?" he asked.

I decided to try out a word that I thought, when spoken just so, sounded terribly British. "Lovely."

He chuckled. "What would you have said if you were in Texas?"

I shrugged. "Awww right." I really drew out and exaggerated the first word.

He laughed and casually put his arm around my shoulders. "I don't know why you don't share that *lovely* accent with everyone."

"It doesn't sound lovely to me," I admitted.

"I suppose beauty is in the ear of the beholder," he remarked.

A bubble of laughter rose in my throat. "I thought it was the eye of the beholder."

"Depends on the beholder and what he's looking for," he teased.

He squeezed my shoulder. My mind said it was a brotherly squeeze, but my heart . . . Well, it seemed it had a *mind* of its own, and it wanted his touch to be so not brotherly.

"Listen, I hope it's okay if you have tea with my mum alone this afternoon. I'd like to spend some time with Brooke," he announced.

Brooke. Oh, I felt like such a fool. Of course. He liked Brooke. Elegant, graceful Brooke. He'd probably wanted to spend time with her yesterday, but he'd had his host sister to contend with.

I shrugged out from under his arm. "No, I don't mind. Go on. Have fun."

He looked guilty, shifting from one foot to the other. "It's just that she was a bit miffed yesterday—"

"Go on," I interrupted. "I understand completely." And unfortunately I did. I could never compete with someone as sophisticated as Brooke.

"I'll see you home first," he offered.

I waved my hand through the air. "Don't be silly. I remember the way, and I'm a big girl. I can get myself home."

"Are you sure?" He had the cutest way of wrinkling his brow. And I really hated for him to feel bad about abandoning me.

"Yeah, I'm sure. I mean, I have to learn my way around sometime. There's no time like the present. You can't rearrange your whole life just because I'm here," I pointed out. Babbling. I was babbling.

He backed up a step. But he didn't look relieved. "Then I'll see you at home later."

"Later," I repeated as cheerfully as I could.

But watching him hurry off to be with Brooke, I'd never felt more miserable.

"Brooke is such a lovely girl," Mrs. Marlin said.

There was that word again: *lovely*. I decided I was going to erase it from my vocabulary.

I had tried to show proper enthusiasm when Mrs. Marlin taught me how to make scones, but the truth was that I wanted to retreat to my room and brood. What was the advantage to living with a cute guy if he had a girlfriend? And as a guy, he wasn't much help when it came to teaching me to be a proper English girl.

"Try the strawberries and cream," Mrs. Marlin suggested.

The cream was actually whipped cream. I took a bite of the scone and shoveled a strawberry and some cream into my mouth. Pretty tasty. I swallowed and smiled. "It's good."

"I've always enjoyed my afternoon tea with Kit," Mrs. Marlin remarked wistfully. "I suppose I need to get used to his wanting to spend the afternoon with a girl other than his mum."

Using my spoon, I made little mountains with the whipped cream in my bowl. "I guess he and Brooke have been going together for a long time."

Mrs. Marlin wrinkled her brow in a way that reminded me of Kit. "Not so long, really. They went out a few times before she went off on holiday, and he seemed rather fond of her then."

Rather fond? I thought of the knee-melting kiss I had witnessed the day before. They were more than fond of each other.

Mrs. Marlin tapped the table. "All done here. I'd best see to dinner."

I helped her clean up before retreating to my room. Sitting at the dainty desk, my laptop humming, I read the e-mail from my mom, really disappointed that I didn't have anything from Dana or Carrie waiting for me.

From: FarmLady
Sent: Tuesday, September 5, 2000, 5:34 A.M.
To: RobininLondon
Subject: We miss you

> Hi, sweetie. Your dad and I sure do miss you. It's so quiet around here. Your dad is still worried that you'll change, but, well . . . It's okay if you do. A farm life isn't for everyone. Robin, I want you to experience everything you can this year. Grow into the girl that you want to be and know that we'll always love you.
>
> —Mom

I could picture my mom sitting at my dad's computer in his untidy office. Her tears would be hitting the keyboard. My mom cried more than anyone I knew. She cried when a horse foaled. She cried when my pigs got first-place ribbons at the county fair. She'd cried at the airport when we said good-bye. And I knew she'd cry the next time I saw her. She was just like that.

My computer spoke to me. "You have mail."

I clicked the mailbox icon. I was thrilled to see that I had mail from Dana.

From: ArtsyDana
Sent: Tuesday, September 5, 2000, 5:00 P.M.
To: RobininLondon, PizzaGirl
Subject: Paris

Robin and Carrie:

You're not going to believe who's in Paris at my school. Alex Johnson! That's right. The same boring Alex Johnson from Mustang High. I'm constantly running into him. He is rapidly becoming the bane of my existence. How can I meet a French guy and fall in love when Alex keeps getting in the way?

And the French guys are to die for. Cute, cute, cute. I've already branded a couple as potential boyfriend candidates. Paris is the most magical place ever. Did you know they have bakeries on almost every corner?

—Au revoir, Dana

I sympathized with Dana. The whole point in joining the YA program was to get away from people we knew. I couldn't remember much about Alex Johnson, so he must not be a guy who made much of an impression. Although Dana was complaining about him, it didn't seem like she was going to let him ruin her year abroad.

My laptop interrupted my thoughts. "You have mail."

I clicked the icon, and there was Carrie's response.

From: PizzaGirl
Sent: Tuesday, September 5, 2000 5:03 P.M.
To: RobininLondon, ArtsyDana
Subject: An experiment in Rome

Alex Johnson? What's he doing there? Never mind. But boring? Alex Johnson? I always thought he was cool. Good luck with the French guys!

Italy is amazing! I've got a little experiment going with an Italian guy. Let's just say that he needed to learn a lesson, and I decided that I was the one to teach it to him. Details to follow.

Hey, Robin, how's that hot "brother" of yours? Any more close encounters? If so, send us the details!

—Ciao, Carrie

I could actually hear Carrie laughing when she wrote the letter. Oh, that felt good, to read letters from my mom and friends. Even though we were in different countries, we were still close. The power of the Internet.

Carrie and Dana sounded so happy, like they were fitting in. Why couldn't I?

I missed home: the farm, my pet pigs, my family, school, the warm Texas weather. And I missed something else, something I couldn't put my finger on.

It was almost as if I missed me, but that couldn't be it because I was here.

I knew I needed to e-mail everyone back, but I didn't want anyone to read any unhappiness into my tone, especially my mom. Before I replied to their e-mails, I needed to work off some tension. Usually I rode my horse, Dreamer, when I was feeling all knotted up like this. Gosh, I missed that mare. Guess I'd have to settle for a walk.

When I strolled into the hallway, I noticed the door to Kit's room was open. I glanced inside, hoping he was home already. But no such luck. He and Brooke were probably caught up in the whirlwind of a heavy make-out session. I spotted a soccer ball in the corner and decided that was exactly what I needed. Something I could kick and vent my frustrations on.

I snatched up the ball and headed out into the garden. I'd played a little soccer with Carrie and her brothers, so I knew to use the side of my foot instead of my toe to dribble the ball. I couldn't do the impressive moves that they could, but my skill was passable enough that her brothers fought over which one would have me on their team.

Carrie was always complaining about her brothers, but I thought they were neat. They were always throwing their arms around my shoulders and rubbing their knuckles on top of my head. I guess it could get old if I was around them and they did it all the time, but it still made me feel special.

Just like Kit had this afternoon. Based on my experiences with Carrie's brothers, however, I should have definitely recognized a brotherly hug when I got one.

Dribbling the soccer ball up and down the garden didn't take much concentration.

Brooke's regal face popped into my mind. I thought about the icy glare she'd given me today when I walked into creative-writing class. Much colder than the one she'd given me yesterday. For a minute I'd been tempted to come home and get my parka. What was it with her and the chilling looks? Why was Brooke being so unfriendly?

It wasn't that the girl could be jealous or insecure that a girl was living in her boyfriend's house. After all, it was just me, hardly someone to inspire jealousy!

I supposed I could ask Kit what Brooke's deal was, but asking obnoxious questions just because I was dying for the answer wasn't appropriate. I'd learned that lesson over and over with Jason. Especially on that most humiliating day of my life, the day I'd realized how embarrassing my real personality was. I shook my head to clear it of the painful memory.

But it didn't work. Why couldn't the brain function like an Etch-A-Sketch? A good, hard shake and everything was erased forever.

Unexpectedly the soccer ball was snatched away, and I staggered forward because I'd set myself up to kick something that was no longer there.

I spun around. Kit stood nearby, holding the ball, a watchful expression on his face.

"Did you have a nice time with your girl-friend?" I asked in a formal tone. He angled his head slightly, and I thought of the look my golden retriever gave me at home—as if he couldn't quite figure out what humans were all about.

Why couldn't I sound like other people when they spoke formally instead of coming across as someone trying to speak formally but failing?

Suddenly Kit smiled, a challenging glint in his eyes that I didn't quite trust. He ignored my question and bounced the ball off his knee. "Let's have a go at a game." He pointed. "That end of the garden is your goal. All you have to do is kick the ball against the fence to score." His smile broadened.

"After you steal it away from me, that is."

With one quick movement he dropped the ball to the ground and began dribbling it toward the other end of the yard—garden. The sneak!

I released a shriek and hightailed it after him. Since he was taller than me, his legs were longer and he could cover ground faster. But I wasn't going to let that little advantage stop me from scoring. Somehow I managed to get in front of him. He turned. I scrambled. He turned again, and amazingly enough—I was ready.

I shot out my foot, hooked my instep around the curve of the ball, and was off.

"Hey!" he yelled, clearly incensed at my agility.

I laughed as I neared the other side. I could feel him bearing down on me, and I gave the ball one hard kick.

It bounced off the fence, the echo of victory reverberating in the air.

"Yeah!" I leaped in the air, and then I did a little dance around the ball like the St. Louis Rams' players did when they got a touchdown, pointing my index fingers at the ball.

Kit picked up the ball. "Let's see you do that again."

"No problem," I goaded, feeling good. Oh, so good.

He dropped the ball to the ground and nudged it forward with his foot. I sidled around. He twisted first one way, then the other, apparently not in any hurry to get it down to his end.

I was impressed with the fancy footwork that always managed to snatch the ball just beyond my reach. I was also highly aggravated by it. It seemed Kit was as competitive as I was. I figured he hoped to wear me out. Only he didn't know the kind of stamina a farm girl built up over the years. My advantage: He didn't know I was a farm girl.

I quickly dodged in front of him and made contact with the ball. But before I could actually say I had possession of it, he had it back.

He darted to the side. I stayed as close as his shadow. My foot hit the ball. His foot hit the ball. Then somehow we both hit the ball, it spiraled upward, our feet got tangled together, and we both lost our balance with a flailing of arms.

Kit groaned as he hit the ground. I yelped when I landed on top of him.

I was certain that I'd had the wind knocked out of me. That was the only logical explanation for the fact that I couldn't breathe. My inability to draw air into my lungs had nothing to do with the fact that I was lying on top of Kit, staring into his deep blue eyes.

"Sorry for tripping you," he mumbled.

"No problem." I was surprised that he was breathing as harshly as I was. But we'd been running, kicking the ball. It was only natural for us to be out of breath.

My hand was pressed to his chest, and I could feel his heart thudding. I wondered if he could hear mine. It was the exercise, not the closeness of each other, that had our hearts racing. At least, that's what I tried to convince myself of.

"Interesting way to play football," a feminine voice announced.

I jerked my head around. Brooke stood over us, her hands planted firmly on her hips.

And she didn't look happy. "Or what do you Americans call it, 'soccer?'"

Ten

Kit

I T WAS BAD form when you had a girlfriend to be caught lying on the ground with another girl in your arms. Unfortunately, at that moment I found myself sort of wishing that I didn't have a girlfriend.

I hadn't quite figured out yet exactly how I felt about Brooke. I'd really been surprised by how glad I was to see her that first day at school. And spending time with her after school, looking through the photos she'd taken while she was in Europe, had been interesting.

Although not as interesting as playing football with Robin.

Awkwardly, Robin and I managed to untangle ourselves. My heart went out to her. Her cheeks were burning a bright crimson. I knew she was embarrassed, and she really had no reason to be. We'd both gotten carried away, playing quite aggressively, which had surprised me. I had never expected Robin to be so . . . animated.

As soon as I was standing, Brooke moved up against me and plopped my Texas Rangers baseball cap on top of my head. "You left this at my house."

I grabbed the bill and settled the cap more firmly into place. I enjoyed watching American baseball and had ordered the cap through the Internet. I didn't wear it often, which was the reason I'd forgotten it. I wasn't even sure why I'd stuffed it into my backpack this morning. Maybe to be closer to my American sister?

"If you'll excuse me," Robin announced formally, "I need to get started on my homework."

I watched her walk into the house with her back straight as a board. I was baffled by the abrupt change in her attitude. She was extremely stiff and distant once again. While we had been playing football, she was exactly as I'd expected an American to be—yelling at me, laughing loudly. And her little tribal dance around the ball had been incredibly cute. Her excitement had been contagious and part of the reason we had gotten tangled up and ended up tripping over our feet.

I hadn't been paying attention to what I'd been doing. I'd been paying attention to her, thoroughly enjoying a girl who was an absolute stranger.

It was almost like there were two Robins—the

one who lived in my house and the one who played soccer. Was it possible her accent wasn't the only thing she wanted to hide?

Robin had barely disappeared into the house before Brooke kissed me. Unexpectedly, just like she had at school. The odd passion almost seemed forced, desperate, not real. I couldn't explain it.

Brooke leaned back and looked up at me. She really was pretty. Blond hair, every strand in place.

"Let's set up Robin with a guy and double-date," she suggested, a twinkle in her green eyes. "Wouldn't that be fun?"

I was incredibly confused. Two different Robins. And now two different Brookes. The one I'd come to know through e-mails this summer and this one standing beside me.

This Brooke was suddenly acting more interesting: kissing me in a very PDA way, suggesting blind dates for Robin, and coming over unexpectedly to return a stupid cap.

Maybe it was wrong not to give her a chance. That sounded rather like an excuse, I realized. But for what? It wasn't as if I was interested in Robin. She was like my sister, for goodness sake. I wasn't really "allowed" to like her.

Still, I didn't want to fix up any of my friends with Robin. If she kissed as passionately as she'd played soccer just then, I didn't want any of my friends to know it.

★   ★   ★

After Brooke left—which wasn't until she'd sold me on this crazy double-date idea—I bounded up the stairs, grabbed my PalmPilot, and went to Robin's room. The open door beckoned me inside, so I didn't bother to knock. She sat on the window seat, a textbook balanced on her knees, but she was looking out the window, a wistful sort of expression on her face.

As I stepped closer, she must have heard me because she turned and gave me a smile that nearly knocked me over. It was like the smile she'd worn when she'd played football. Only it was warmer. Had I really thought when I first met her that she was afraid to smile?

I realized now that she had probably only been nervous that first night. And that was certainly understandable. A new home, new people, new country.

I'd never realized before how quickly I judged people. First Brooke and now Robin. I hadn't given myself a chance to really get to know either one of them. I was glad now that Brooke had suggested the double date. It would be fun.

I thought about sitting on the window seat, but after getting so close to her when we had played football earlier, I thought it would be best if I kept my distance a bit. So I just stood where I'd stopped when she flashed that beautiful smile at me. "I hope I didn't hurt you earlier when we fell."

Her smile deepened, and her cheeks burned a bright red. "Naw, I'm pretty tough."

Her accent reminded me of a slowly sung ballad. When she spoke naturally, it was as if the words weren't in any hurry to get anywhere. I found it incredibly appealing.

"Right. I'm glad to hear that." I held up my PalmPilot. "I thought we'd double-date Sunday afternoon. I need to compile a list of your likes and dislikes so I can accurately match you up with one of my friends."

The smile abruptly left her face, the blush turned a deeper red, and she stared at me with large, round blue eyes. "I'm not ready for a date. I—I won't be ready for months," she stammered.

Huh? What did she mean by that?

She set the book aside, scrambled off the window seat, and began to pace agitatedly. "You see, I feel it's important to acclimate myself to London first, become one with the culture, make friends, then maybe worry about dating."

She was moving her arms through the air like a Dutch windmill.

"I just got out of a relationship back home, and I need the break anyway." She gave a quick nod, and her hands stilled.

She's lying, I thought. I wasn't sure about which part, but I could sense from her body language and the way she'd rushed around like she was trying to escape from her words that she was lying.

I rocked back on my heels. "All right, then. How about if Brooke and I, plus you and one of my mates, all go out Sunday? Just chums getting together?"

She hesitated. I was fascinated, watching her. I thought I could actually see her carrying on an argument with herself. She finally nodded. "Okay."

I was surprised by the depth of my relief. She wasn't into dating! Great! Any of my friends would be crazy about her: She was so pretty, caring, and fun.

I'd seen that from a distance when she was at the Tower of London with her friends. There seemed to be so many facets to her personality. Suddenly I realized that if she wasn't into dating, she'd also not be interested in dating me.

I crashed for a second, then realized that didn't matter because we were like brother and sister. We lived in the same house.

We couldn't date, could we?

The next day at school I studied my friends. Which one should I ask to be Robin's nondate?

I wanted someone on the good-looking side, but he didn't have to be movie-star handsome. He needed to be fairly intelligent. Based on the snatches of conversation I'd overhead at the Tower, I knew Robin was no slouch in the intelligence department. Besides, the YA student was expected to make certain marks in school, so I figured she did well at her studies.

I thought of the way she'd gotten upset over the ravens' wings being clipped. Her nondate should be compassionate.

I remembered the absolutely terrific way she'd laughed when I'd made my comment about the guard's Mickey Mouse ears. She did have a sense of humor. It just didn't surface often, so I wanted her nondate to have a sense of humor as well.

Using my PalmPilot, I ticked off the traits I thought would appeal to her. Unfortunately, the most practical choice wasn't the best choice: me!

Right. So I probably wasn't going to be able to settle on one of my mates who had all the traits I thought she'd admire in a bloke, but surely someone had most of the traits.

Throughout the morning, in the hallways and in our creative-writing class, I noticed that lots of guys checked her out and seemed interested in getting to know her. Several of them asked her questions, but she always shied away. It was a cute maneuver she'd perfected. Ducking her head slightly, smiling shyly, and scurrying away as soon as she'd quickly answered whatever the question had been. Good. It didn't seem like anyone had caught her fancy.

I knew I shouldn't be glad, but I was.

When I sat beside Brooke at lunch, I was no closer to selecting the perfect nondate than I had been when I began this mission. I brought out my PalmPilot and studied my list of requisites.

"What are you doing?" Brooke inquired.

"Still trying to determine who would be a good date for Robin," I replied.

She scoffed. "What's to decide? Ask the next guy you pass in the hallway."

I scowled at her. "She's my sister, Brooke. You don't set your sister up with just anyone."

Richard Wiggins dropped into the chair across from me. We'd been friends forever. "How's it going with the YAS?" he asked.

I glared at him. "She has a name. It's Robin."

He looked taken aback, and I immediately regretted my outburst.

"What's wrong with you?" Brooke demanded. "He was just being polite."

"I'm sorry, Richard." I truly was. "It's just that everyone keeps calling her the YAS as though she's a thing. And she's a person with thoughts, feelings, fears, dreams—"

"Whoa!" Brooke interrupted me. "This is getting a little too heavy."

"Again, I apologize." How could I explain the responsibility I felt as Robin's brother? "I've never been a brother before."

"Sounds like you're taking the role way too seriously, man," Richard informed me.

I released a nervous chuckle. "Probably."

"How about Richard?" Brooke asked.

"Richard?" I stared at her, flustered.

She nodded. "As a possible date for Robin."

I jerked my gaze to Richard. With his brown hair and eyes, he was really better looking than what I had in mind. On the other hand, I did enjoy his company, so it was likely that Robin would too.

Hmmm. Why did that thought bother me? It shouldn't. After all, this wasn't really a date.

Brooke reached across the table and took Richard's hand. I didn't know if I'd ever seen a guy blush before.

"We're looking for someone to date Robin," Brooke explained.

"Not a real date," I hastily added.

Brooke snapped her attention to me. "What?"

"Well, Robin doesn't feel that she's acclimated enough for a real date, so all we really want is someone to sort of serve as her escort Sunday afternoon," I clarified.

Richard shrugged. "Sure. Sounds like it might be jolly good fun."

Of course it would be, I thought. And I could trust Richard. He wouldn't come on overly strong or make Robin feel uncomfortable. Besides, Robin would be too shy and reserved to attract Richard anyway. Right?

Plus Robin wasn't into dating. No problem.

Eleven

Robin

BY SUNDAY AFTERNOON I was an absolute basket case about my first date, unofficial or not. Brooke hated me, Kit was probably hoping I'd hit it off with Richard so I'd take the pressure off him to be my "host brother," and Richard would probably be unable to hear a word I spoke because I'd be trying to hide my stupid accent!

I pulled a soft-knit, light blue turtleneck sweater over my head. I wished I could just go out with Kit and talk to him about what I was trying to do and why.

I looked in the mirror and used my fingers to fluff up my hair. Kit was so easy to talk to, and he wasn't judgmental at all. But then in order to explain what I wanted to be, I'd have to admit what I truly was.

111

I moved closer to the mirror and applied a light layer of lip gloss that was almost the shade of my lips. It didn't really add a lot of color, but it managed to highlight them a little. I didn't even know why I was so worried about the way my lips looked. It wasn't as if any guy was dying to press his mouth to mine.

Suddenly images flashed through my mind— like previews of past attractions.

I thought about those heavenly moments when Kit and I had been lying on the ground together, entangled in what could have so easily turned into a kiss. Our eyes had been locked on each other, our mouths scant inches apart. I'd felt his warm breath whispering over my cheek. If he'd just shifted a little, the kiss would have become reality instead of just living in my imagination.

Yeah, right. While we'd been playing soccer, I'd practically blown my cover. My face burned every time I thought about that ridiculous dance I did around the soccer ball. He'd laughed, and I'd loved the sound of his laughter. But no guy wanted to get involved with a girl that he laughed at.

So forget it. I couldn't let Kit know the real me. Even though he had a perfect girlfriend, and Kit and I were just friends, I still couldn't bear for him to think of me the way Jason had.

I sat in the movie theater, grateful for the darkness. Richard was on my left. Kit on my right. And elegant Brooke was on the other side of Kit.

I was certain that my face was still red.

When we were riding the tube, Brooke had suggested that we go to Piccadilly Circus. I'd gotten really excited at the prospect of seeing animals perform. I had actually thought that I might have something in common with these people.

"I love the circus," I'd announced in a moderate but stately tone. "We always go see Ringling Brothers' when they're in the area."

Brooke had stared at me, obviously in shock that I had spoken. "You're kidding us, right?"

Richard had looked like he wished he was anywhere but sitting next to me.

Kit had given me an embarrassing kind of grimace as though he hated to break the news to me. "Piccadilly Circus is what we call the entrance to the entertainment district."

I had tried to salvage my pride and make light of my ignorance. "No high-wire acts, then?"

He had grinned. "Sorry."

So now I sat straight and tall in the theater when I really wanted to slouch down in my seat until I was invisible. But in the back of my mind, I heard Carrie and Dana daring me to see this through to the end.

I cast a sideways glance at Richard. His brown hair was spiked in the front, short on the sides, and long in the back. He was cute, and even though this was a nondate, he'd bought my ticket and popcorn.

Unfortunately, I only remembered he was here when I thought about it. Kit—I was constantly aware of him sitting beside me.

He shifted in his seat, and his arm touched mine where it lay on the armrest. I thought about how wonderful it would be if he turned over his hand and wrapped his fingers around mine.

Like he would ever want to hold my hand. Especially when he was sitting next to gorgeous Brooke. I slid my gaze past him to Brooke. From the moment we'd arrived at her house, I'd been watching her closely. I pretty much had her I-can't-believe-you-actually-said-that look down pat. She must have given it to me at least a half dozen times. Pretty much any time that I spoke.

When she wasn't looking at me with a frigid glare, she was actually worth studying. Her walk was kinda slinky, seamless. And she did this little flip with her hair that made her shoulders roll. She spoke softly but was still audible. I realized that was where I'd made my mistake. Trying to talk quietly. I just needed to talk softly.

Yeah, right. Breaking Brooke down into parts was like missing the forest for the trees. Overall, she was like a national forest—not just a solitary oak tree.

Brooke was so perfect that she was intimidating. And she did it without trying.

★   ★   ★

As we stepped out of the theater, I was again hit by the life that pulsed through Piccadilly Circus. It was late afternoon, but bright neon lights advertised Coca-Cola, McDonald's, Sanyo, and other products—British and non-British. It was amazing. It was like a melting pot of products. We had nothing like it in Mustang, and I was awestruck as we passed restaurant after restaurant.

My traitorous gaze kept returning to Kit and Brooke, walking in front of Richard and me. K & B—as I was beginning to think of them—were holding hands and talking with their heads bent and close to each other. Then Kit laughed. The sound washed over me, and I remembered how much he'd laughed during our little soccer game.

He hadn't laughed much since. But then, being funny wasn't what I wanted.

I glanced over at Richard. He was shuffling along beside me, his hands shoved in the pockets of his baggy jeans, his eyes focused on K & B too. I wondered what he was thinking. I thought about asking but figured being nosy wasn't too sophisticated.

Kit turned slightly, grinned broadly, and jerked his thumb toward a restaurant. "Fish-and-chips?"

"Sounds good," Richard replied.

I thought of cornmeal-covered catfish fried in huge barrels of grease at family reunions. I'd avoided American foods since I'd arrived, but something with a back-home taste appealed to me as we walked into the restaurant.

We sat in a corner booth. I could look out the window and see everyone hurrying by. I saw a lot of couples, and I wondered how long it would take for me to learn everything I needed to capture a guy's attention.

I certainly didn't seem to have Richard's. He was studying the tines on his fork like he wasn't quite sure what they were used for.

The waitress came over to take our order.

"Fish-and-chips all around," Kit told her. "And cola."

When she had walked away, Kit tapped his fingers on the table and looked at me. "Did you enjoy the film?"

"What I could understand," I admitted. It had been a British movie.

"There was a lot of cockney in it," Kit explained. "There are a variety of accents in Britain, and you can usually tell where someone is from based on their accent."

"Texas is like that," I told him.

Brooke did that little flip of her hair and settled her gaze on me. "I thought you'd sound like J. R. Ewing, but you don't have any accent." One night Kit and I had watched reruns of the old *Dallas* series. It seemed a lot of American shows were in syndication over here. "All your words sound exactly the same, a steady sound," Brooke continued.

I couldn't have been more pleased that I'd managed to effectively eliminate the twang in my words.

Brooke wrinkled her nose. "You know. Like the constant beep on a heart monitor after the patient has died."

That stung. "I don't have much of an accent because I'm from the city." And I was working like crazy not to reveal my drawl.

"Her friends are from the country and have really cute accents," Kit told Brooke. He looked at Richard. "They actually say y'all."

Brooke shook her head. "I'm sure they were putting that on."

"No, they weren't," Kit insisted. "When we were at the Tower, they were saying it all the time, and I knew they weren't thinking about it."

Thank goodness, the waitress arrived with our orders right then, so the subject of accents got dropped. She set my plate in front of me. I picked up a big, fat, juicy french fry. I smiled at the waitress. "I was expecting potato chips."

She rolled her eyes.

Brooke shook her head in agreement. "That's so typically American."

"That makes sense since I'm a typical American," I shot back. I was getting fighting mad. I couldn't understand why Brooke felt this need to throw constant jabs my way. What had I done to her? Other than move in with her boyfriend, that is.

We ate without talking. Instead of ketchup everyone soaked their fish-and-chips in malt vinegar. It gave it a certain tangy taste that appealed to me.

But the heavy silence weaving itself around us was enough to ruin my appetite. I ate only half the food on my plate.

I glanced at Richard. He was staring at Brooke. He shifted his gaze to me and, with a guilty look, he went back to munching his fries. When he was finished eating, he patted his stomach. "That hit the spot."

He cast a quick glance at Brooke again.

I wished I knew how to liven up the group. I thought about all the times Carrie, Dana, and I went out to eat. The conversation and laughter were nonstop.

Kit reached across the table and jabbed Richard lightly on the shoulder. "Why don't you and Robin go put on some music?"

Richard looked at me and shrugged. "Sure."

He scooted out of the booth. Without giving a backward glance to Brooke, I followed. I wondered if Kit wanted to get rid of us so he could tell his nasty girlfriend to be nicer on the trip home. Or were they going to laugh at me?

We got to the jukebox. Richard slipped some coins into the slot. "Punch the ones you want."

He cast a quick glance at our table. I figured he

wasn't looking at Kit. *Why would any English guy like uncouth me?* I thought sadly.

Even though this was a nondate, I felt like a zero. "Which ones do you like?" I prodded.

He looked surprised that I'd spoken. Then he gave me a small smile. "You know? You do have an accent when you're angry."

"I'm not angry." I leaned my hip against the jukebox. "This whole nondate thing is just kinda awkward."

He nodded. "Yeah. I've never gone out with a girl before that I wasn't supposed to like."

I stared at him. "You're not supposed to like me?"

"Well, you know, not in a date kind of way," he explained.

I laughed. "Yeah, right." I looked at the list of songs. "Why don't you pick them?" It only seemed fair since it was his money.

"All right, I will."

He went to studying the songs, and I cast a quick glance back at our table. Kit's eyes were glued to Brooke's face. It sure didn't look like he was giving her a dressing-down. As they talked, he tucked a strand of hair behind her ear.

Okay, so he just wanted to be alone with her. I felt like the third wheel on a bicycle.

'N Sync began singing "Bye Bye Bye." I remembered Carrie's excitement the day she got their *No Strings Attached* CD. She'd had a sleep over, and she'd played the thing all night.

Suddenly I wanted to be back home, curled up on my bed, talking to my friends, staring at a room that was all me with county-fair ribbons hanging on the wall.

I had been crazy to think hillbilly, country-hick-farm-girl me could survive in London.

Richard slapped his palms against the jukebox. "There we go. You pick the last one."

Without looking, I just punched a number. I was really starting to hate this whole nondate idea.

Richard and I returned to the booth. Brooke was snuggled against Kit now. His arm was along the back of the booth, his fingers toying with her blond strands. I felt pathetic noticing all this and wishing I was sitting on the other side of the booth exactly where Brooke was.

"What's everyone planning for their oral presentation for the creative-writing class?" Brooke asked.

I'd been doing all I could to avoid thinking about the presentation. Having it slapped in front of me, plus the whole horrible nondate, made me really queasy. I broke out in a light, cold sweat, and I actually thought I might throw up.

Richard touched my shoulder. "Hey, you look a little pale. Are you okay?"

I forced myself to give him a shaky smile. "I'm not used to pouring vinegar on my food. I think I used too much. I'm kind of nauseated. I hate to be a party pooper, but maybe I should just go home."

Great. Now I'd just told everyone the state of my stomach. That was real sophisticated.

I thought the ride home on the tube would never end. Everyone was silent, and I was reminded of deathbed scenes from movies. I just didn't think this night could get any worse.

I was wrong.

Kit and Brooke stood at the end of the sidewalk while Richard walked me to the door. In silence.

I couldn't believe it when he leaned forward and kissed me—a small peck on the cheek. I imagined he was Kit, and that was so totally unfair to Richard.

But I was feeling miserable. Physically and emotionally.

"I'm sorry I ended the night so soon." I glanced at my watch. "It's barely six-thirty." We'd caught an early afternoon movie.

Richard shrugged. "Don't worry about it. It's not a problem."

"Guess I'll—I'll see you around," I stammered, trying to find a way to make a quick getaway.

"Sure thing. Cheerio, then." He turned and hurried to join his friends.

I watched Kit, Brooke, and Richard start walking away. I figured the three of them were going to go back out for a night on the town now that I'd made it easy for them to get rid of the hick.

Twelve

Kit

I DIDN'T SAY much as we walked Richard home. Brooke was between us, her arms linked around mine and Richard's. I felt rather like the characters out of *The Wizard of Oz,* trudging down the yellow brick road.

Brooke was telling Richard that he was really a good sport to suffer through an afternoon excursion with the American.

"She's not half bad," Richard commented.

Not half bad? Then why bother to kiss her!

I was surprised how much I had disliked watching Richard lean close and give Robin a kiss. Even though it was just on the cheek, he'd gotten closer than I'd thought he should. I wanted to ask him if her cheek was as soft as it looked. If her breath had caught. If her eyes had twinkled or darkened with passion.

Passion for a kiss on the cheek? I was totally losing it. I shouldn't even care.

Brooke leaned into Richard and laughed lightly. "You're so gallant."

Richard latched his gaze onto hers with something close to adoration—like she'd just knighted him or some such. Then he looked at me, and his face turned red. He shrugged as if he was suddenly embarrassed. "I'm not gallant. I was just doing my good mate here a favor."

What was going on? I had noticed him looking at Brooke a couple of times, but I couldn't fault him for that. I'd seldom been able to keep my eyes off Robin. It was a natural guy thing to compare your date against the other guy's. Only this hadn't been a date!

I'd kept telling myself that I was just watching Robin to make sure she had a good time. Brothers are supposed to do that. Although I felt guilty because if I was honest with myself, I really hadn't wanted her to have a good time. Not with Richard anyway.

We finally arrived at Richard's house. He worked his way out of the pretzel twist Brooke had on his arm.

"Thanks for going with us," I told him.

"Sure, it was fun," he commented. "See you around."

He disappeared into his house, and I chalked up the afternoon as one of the most miserable of my life. Now I just needed to get Brooke home, and then I could go check on Robin. I felt bad that she wasn't feeling well, like it was somehow my fault.

Brooke leaned her head against my arm. "Why don't we go back to your house to watch a video on the telly?"

Although I wanted to look in on Robin, I didn't want to do it with Brooke there. Yet Brooke was my steady, and it wasn't right to make her play second fiddle just because I suddenly found myself with a sister who intrigued me.

"Why don't we go to your house?" I suggested.

She wrinkled her nose and tightened her hold on my arm. "My parents have people over. We wouldn't have any privacy."

Privacy. We definitely needed some privacy. Most of the time I liked Brooke a great deal. But sometimes . . . I couldn't quite put my finger on what it was about her that bothered me. I hadn't liked some of the things she'd said to Robin, but I chalked it up to an overly protective brotherly instinct. I was, after all, new at this being-a-brother stuff.

As we turned toward my house, I felt funny taking Brooke back over there with Robin not feeling well upstairs, but maybe time alone on my own turf with Brooke would be a good way to determine exactly how I felt around her.

If I could figure out how I felt about Brooke,

maybe I'd understand why I spent so much time thinking about Robin.

I sat on the sofa with Brooke snuggled against my side.

I figured it was because I'd watched *The Sixth Sense* close to a dozen times, trying to discern all the subtle hints in the movie, that my mind wandered now. It just couldn't hold my attention any longer since I could practically recite the dialogue line by line.

I'd wanted to pop upstairs to check on Robin, but Brooke was being very possessive. She'd explained to me that when a girl wasn't feeling well, the last thing she wanted was for some guy to see her. Only I wasn't *some* guy. I was her brother.

But Brooke convinced me that it just wasn't done. Since she had two sisters and no brothers, I wasn't certain how she'd learned this bit of information, but the last thing I wanted to do was offend Robin. She had somehow, amazingly, in a short time become very important to me. I wanted everything to be absolutely wonderful for her. And I just didn't know how to make that happen.

Brooke wiggled against me as if we didn't fit together quite right and she couldn't find a comfortable spot. I really liked the way she felt against me, though. I liked her soft perfume and the way her silky hair felt as I toyed with it.

"The double date was an absolute disaster,"

Brooke announced. She'd seen the movie before as well, but it was her idea to watch it again. "Could Robin have done anything else to make it so not fun?"

What I didn't always like were the words that she spoke. The condescending tone of her voice. The way she said Robin's name like it was something to flush down the toilet. I was overwhelmed by the jumble of images her comment caused.

"You don't like Robin, do you?" I accused.

"What's to like? She is so weird. One minute she's a quiet, timid mouse, and the next she's blurting out some dumb comment. Her accent is ridiculous, and you'd think someone would learn the customs and language of another country before coming for a year. She's so embarrassing!"

Red-hot rage surged through me. I'd never in my life felt this angry. I was totally prepared to tell Brooke off and break up with her, but I needed some distance between us so she could feel the full effect of my wrath.

I jumped off the sofa, my arms flailing. Unfortunately, my glass of cola caught the impact of my anger. I sent the glass and its contents flying, and it landed with a thud on my mum's intricate oriental rug.

Blast it all!

That certainly served to quench my fury. My mum was particular about how things looked.

I rushed into the kitchen to grab a dishrag. I stumbled to a stop.

Robin was standing there. Tears welled in her eyes, and her bottom lip trembled. The depth of sadness in her eyes was enormous, and I could envision only one thing that would make her this sad.

She'd heard Brooke.

A tear plopped onto her cheek, and I thought my heart was going to break. I remembered the girl who had tried to talk quietly so no one would know she had such a wonderful accent. An accent she was ashamed of for reasons I couldn't begin to comprehend. I remembered the hurt in her eyes when the guard at the crown jewels had looked down his nose at her.

And somehow I knew instinctively that people saying cruel things to her wasn't new. And Brooke must have listed everything about Robin that she doubted within herself.

But those were just Brooke's words, not my feelings.

I opened my mouth, but before I could utter a word, Robin burst into tears and rushed past me.

"Robin!" I called after her as she ran through the living room and out the front door.

The door slamming echoed around me as I walked into the living room.

Brooke stood and crossed her arms over her

chest. "I'm so glad the crybaby ran away. Maybe she'll learn a lesson about how to act."

At that moment I absolutely lost it. Something I'd never done. Cool, calm Kit faded into the wallpaper, and someone I hardly recognized stood in my shoes.

"You're the one who needs to learn how to act!" I blasted out.

Brooke dropped back down onto the sofa, her eyes and mouth forming large, perfect circles as I marched toward her. With my hands balled into fists at my side, I towered over her. She had to bend back her head to look at me, which I found extremely gratifying.

"Robin is different, yes," I concurred. "Absolutely! No question about it. She's pretty, refreshing, and fun. She looks at London as if everything is wonderful and exciting. She's brave. She's in a foreign country, living in a house with strangers, going to a new school where she doesn't know anyone, and trying her hardest to fit in. I wasn't what she was expecting, but she kept her chin up and accepted it. I would think you would understand. You were in foreign countries this summer. Robin doesn't complain about every little thing like you do. She's loads of fun when you're not around."

Brooke narrowed her eyes and slowly came to her feet like a panther about to strike. "Fine!" she spat. "If she's so wonderful, then date her yourself."

129

"Maybe I will, but one thing is for certain—I'm not dating you any longer. You and I are through." The words just came out and with them, a sense of relief.

Brooke stormed out. I was left standing alone in the living room, the angry words echoing around me.

Full-blown, out-of-control panic was taking hold of me with a vengeance. Night was settling around me, and I couldn't find Robin. I had this horrible vision of her getting lost in the maze of tubes, never finding her way home. Or worse yet, getting off the tube and getting lost in the maze of London streets.

Standing in front of my house, right back where I'd started, I took a shuddering breath. Panic was so totally unlike me. I was literally running around like a chicken with my head cut off. I didn't know where to look. As far as I knew, I was the only friend Robin had in London—and some friend I'd turned out to be. Subjecting her to Brooke's vicious tongue and icy glares.

I wouldn't be surprised if she packed her bags and joined her true friends in Paris or Rome.

That thought caused the panic to recede and sadness to sweep in. I simply couldn't stand the thought of her leaving. Of never again seeing her sit in the window seat or watching her kick a ball around in my mum's garden.

My mum's garden!

Of course. It had to be Robin's favorite spot in London. It was the place where she'd most been herself. She could have easily gone out the front door and circled around to the back.

Sure enough, that was where I found her. Sitting on a bench inside the gazebo, sobbing quietly.

Just like her accent, she wanted to hide her sorrows. And just like I wanted to hear her accent, I wanted to share everything that was bothering her.

I stepped beneath the latticed archway. She glanced up and quickly swiped away the tears on her cheeks. Unfortunately, there were enough left in her eyes to roll over and dampen her cheeks again. I handed her my handkerchief.

"Thanks," she rasped. She wiped her tears and delicately blew her red, swollen nose. Why I would think that nose was cute at this moment was beyond me.

I shoved my hand into my jeans pocket. "I'm sorry you heard all that," I murmured.

She just shook her head, and I saw more tears surface. I felt wholly inadequate at being a brother or being a friend to this American.

"I told Brooke off. I explained in no uncertain terms that everything she said was so far from being right that it made her look petty and—"

"Everything she said is true," Robin interrupted me. "Everything. I've only been in London a week, and already I'm a laughingstock. Even when I try to tone down my accent and be more proper, I come across as *embarrassing!* Maybe I should just go home."

My heart lurched at the thought of her leaving.

"Maybe I'm not cut out for a year abroad," she continued. "Maybe I'm incapable of ever being more than a loudmouth hillbilly."

She released a heart-wrenching sob that made her shoulders quake. I dropped onto the bench beside her, slid my arms around her, and drew her close. It was uncanny the way that her face fit perfectly within the hollow of my shoulder.

"You're not a loudmouthed hillbilly," I reassured her.

"Yes, I am. Jason Turner said so," she lamented.

"Who is Jason Turner?" I wondered aloud. He sounded like a complete idiot.

"He's a guy that went to my school back home." She glanced up at me quickly, then lowered her gaze. "I had a major crush on him. He'd moved to Mustang from Dallas. I figured he didn't know anyone since he was new, so I asked him to go to the county fair with me. He had some excuse, something to do that weekend. But I kept asking him out to other things, and he kept saying no."

"He didn't tell you why?" I asked gently.

She shook her head, burrowing the side of her face more deeply into my shoulder. "Not until I went too far."

"However did you manage to go too far?" I was

definitely confused. All I could see was someone trying to help a stranger feel at home, not unlike what I'd tried to do. Although I'd certainly failed at every turn.

She sniffled. "I approached him in the cafeteria. He was sitting at a table with some people. I asked him if he wanted to go to a mud run with me."

"A mud run?"

She released a tiny chuckle. "You watch big-wheeled trucks race through an obstacle path that's mostly mud and bogs. It can get really exciting."

"It sounds as if it would be," I lied. I decided it was one of those things you had to be there to appreciate. Even though at first mention I didn't find it particularly appealing, I thought attending anything with this girl I held in my arms would be delightful. I would have given it a go had she asked me. "So what happened?" I prodded.

She moved away from me and studied her hands, balled in her lap. "He snapped. He stood up and yelled in front of everyone that I was an obnoxious, annoying, loud, brash pest. He was sick of being embarrassed by me all the time. That he wasn't interested and I'd better get it through my thick skull! That's when I realized how I came across to people. I'm not fun to be around after all. I realized how everyone I dealt with must see me."

I was dumbfounded. "You're only seeing yourself through the eyes of one stupid guy."

133

"No, he was more than that. He came from the city, had seen so much of the world." She shifted on the bench until she faced me. Her eyes held such earnestness. "That's when I came up with my plan to come to London. Everyone here is so sophisticated, so refined. I wanted to spend a year here so I could return to Texas a changed girl: an English girl."

An English girl. I'd just broken up with an English girl—because of this American girl. This American girl who was trying so hard to hide her true self.

"I wish you'd let me see the American girl that you truly are," I pleaded. "The girl you just described sounds like a lot of fun."

She scoffed. "You're just being nice."

"No, honestly, ever since you got here, I've been so intrigued by the girl I've glimpsed those times when you forgot to hide your true self. That's the girl I wish I could have living in my house."

Robin bolted off the bench. Having experienced this same response from Brooke earlier, I knew this action wasn't a good sign. Robin began to pace, her arms flailing about in circles. This was the true Robin, I realized. A girl so enamored of life that she couldn't be still.

"I'm not the girl you caught glimpses of. You haven't seen the real me since I've been here because I've kept her hidden. Believe me, you would detest her as much as Jason did." She stopped pacing and faced me squarely, her hands planted on her hips. "If you were my friend, you'd coach me on the lingo and teach me how to act."

That she wanted to thrust this desire for a transformation on me angered me beyond reason. I stood. "If you really want to turn into a boring, reserved, prissy girl who's unenthusiastic and no fun to be around, I'm not going to help you."

I spun on my heel and headed inside.

Thirteen

Robin

*F*URIOUS WAS TOO tame a word for what I was feeling as I stomped up the stairs to my room.

Who did Kit think he was?

How dare he say such ugly things to me!

I stopped beside his room and glared hard at the closed door. I was surprised that it didn't burst into flames.

I jerked open the door to my room, stalked inside, and slammed the door behind me. The one advantage to my anger was that it had driven away the hurt I'd been feeling earlier.

I began formulating a plan. If Kit wasn't going to help me, I'd just help myself. Besides, who wanted the help of a guy who had absolutely no idea what he was talking about?

He'd like to get to know the real me? Yeah, right. When pigs could fly.

He liked Brooke, for goodness sake! How could he ever like the real me?

I plopped onto the bed, picked up the remote, and turned on the small television that sat on a little table in the corner. I hadn't watched it much while I'd been here. No time, really. While I was running around crazily trying to absorb all the culture, it was sitting right here, waiting for me.

I began flicking the channels. *There are a lot of American TV shows here,* I realized in annoyance.

I finally found an English show. Okay, so the subject was gardening. The host was a woman who spoke with a very charming accent. All I had to do was mimic her.

There was absolutely no way I was going to embarrass myself during that oral presentation tomorrow. I was going to learn to speak and act the way I was expected to: in a reserved, accent-free, proper, elegant way.

The first thing I had to do was lose the twang.

"When pruning roses, you want to make sure that you avoid pricking your fingers on the thorns," the woman said, smiling gently.

That was probably a sentence that I'd never use in my entire life. Even so, I tried it out. "When prunin' roses, you wanna make shore that you avoid prickin' your fingers on the thorns."

I repeated the sentence, listening carefully. I

138

realized I was dropping the *g* when I spoke. While her words ended in a nicely ringing *ing,* mine came to an abrupt halt with *in.* Disgusting. No wonder I sounded hick. I spoke the words in a slow drawl but still managed to cut off part of them. Worse than that, some words like *want to* ended up being one word with no *t* sound whatsoever. I was pathetic, but teachable.

"When prunin' . . . pruning roses, you wanna make sure that you avoid prickin' . . . pricking your fingers on thorns."

I felt like that sentence was filled with thorns. But I repeated it over and over, listening intently to each word until it finally came out: "When pruning roses, you want to make sure that you avoid pricking your fingers on the thorns."

Jolly good show! I thought, knowing now how Eliza Doolittle had felt. I skipped around the room, singing, "The Rain in Spain."

Then I stopped and looked at the girl on the TV. Only the program had changed. Based on the canned laughter, I was watching a comedy, but I couldn't understand most of the words. They spoke so quickly. Was it cockney they were using? I definitely didn't need to pick up another accent.

I switched off the TV and simply recited words I knew that ended in *ing.* As long as I stayed focused, I could speak clearly, succinctly, without a twang reverberating against my eardrums.

I was feeling the panic ebb away.

Now all I needed to do was write out my oral presentation and start practicing in front of the mirror. As much as possible, I needed to avoid including words that ended in *ing*. Sure, I'd mastered not dropping the *g*, but why take chances?

I decided to write about my goal of learning all the English words that are different from American words, like *jumper* for *sweater* and *tube* for *subway*. That way I'd show everyone that I was trying to become a Londoner while in London. Then they could accept me as one of them.

I turned on my laptop and began typing away, carefully wording my presentation so I didn't fall into any hidden traps, words that could foul me up. I spoke out loud as I typed, testing the words, concentrating on no twang.

Preparation was the key.

The phone rang, and I nearly jumped out of my skin. I caught myself just before I picked up the receiver. There was no one here to call me. I went back to working on my presentation. I was actually getting into it. It would help ensure my metamorphosis from Texas Robin into London Robin.

A knock on the door had me hitting the keys so that a string of *z*s flew across my screen. I really wasn't in the mood to talk to Kit.

"Robin?"

Ah, it was Mrs. Marlin.

I jumped up and opened the door. "Yes, ma'am?" Inwardly I cringed. Definitely a drawl on *ma'am*.

"Phone call for you."

Joy surged through me. It had to be my mom. "Thanks."

I closed the door and hurried to the phone. "Howdy!"

"Robin?" a deep voice inquired, definitely not my mom. I grimaced. My greeting had been about as Texas as I could get.

"Yes," I replied very succinctly.

"It's Richard."

Knock me over with a feather. I dropped into a chair. "Hi."

"Listen, I was wondering if you'd like to go to the school social with me tomorrow night," he announced.

Whoa! This was a total shock. I'd gotten the impression that Richard didn't even like me. Why would he invite me to the social? Still, I wanted to experience London life, so I said, "Sure. I'd love to."

"Great! I'll drop round your house at seven," he said.

Then he hung up. *Bam!*

That was weird. *Maybe I did okay tonight after all.*

Yeah, that was it, I thought. I did okay, and maybe Richard was surprised. After all, they told him not to like me as a date, but obviously he did.

That just went to show how wrong Kit was. Thanks to me trying my hardest to be different, I now had a date to the social.

Feeling better about everything, I began working to finish my presentation. But I kept getting distracted.

The guy I really wanted to go to the social with thought I was a total idiot—without even seeing the real me at work!

Kit just didn't get it, I thought sadly.

I wondered if he'd apologize to Brooke for giving her what for and take her to the social. Probably. Now they could both laugh at how ridiculous I was.

Fourteen

Kit

LYING ON MY bed, I stared gloomily at the ceiling and wondered if Robin was still talking to Richard on the phone.

I really owed Richard one.

After that horrible argument with Robin downstairs, I'd called him.

"Hey, Richard, I've got a major favor to ask," I'd told him as soon as he answered the phone.

"Ask away, buddy," he responded.

I took a deep breath before I blurted out, "I need you to take Robin to the school social tomorrow night."

"You're kidding, right?" he scoffed.

"I'm serious. I know things didn't go splendidly today—"

"That's an understatement," he interrupted. "I

can't hear half of what she says. And when I can hear her, what she does say is just plain weird."

"It's simply because she's nervous, being in a strange country and all," I tried to explain. That was partly true, although Robin would be nervous no matter where she was. That much had become obvious in the gazebo. I thought it was a real shame too.

"Ask someone else," Richard responded.

"Come on, Richard, be a good sport. She's the YAS. Taking her to the social will elevate your status in the school," I pointed out. Not that Richard needed his status elevated. Everyone pretty much liked him, and I figured he could really go out with any girl he wanted. I could almost hear the wheels turning in his head as he mulled that over. I needed to strike quickly and deadly. "I promise I'll do any favor you ask in the future."

"Any favor?" he asked, skepticism evident in his voice.

"Any favor at all without hesitation," I promised.

"All right, then, I'll do it."

Two minutes after we hung up, the phone rang for Robin, and I knew Richard was inviting her to the social.

I knew that Richard was the kind of guy Robin wanted or hoped to impress with the new her. I might not agree with what she was doing, but I did want her to be happy.

It's not like she'd go with me, I reminded myself. *She pretty much hates my guts now.*

I'd never felt so much internal conflict. I wanted her to like me, but I knew that I could never like the girl she wanted to become.

All in all, though, by calling Richard, I knew I'd done a good thing by Robin. I rolled over in bed, pounded my fist into my pillow, and tried to fall asleep.

But that wasn't likely to happen.

The next morning I sat on the edge of the mattress and hung my head.

I had no idea what sort of reception I'd get from Robin. I'd actually considered sneaking off to school and sparing her my presence. I was probably the worst excuse for a brother that ever lived.

Of course, the problem was that I really didn't want to be her brother.

I looked at my clock. The minutes were ticking by. She hadn't knocked on my door. She was usually pretty punctual about getting in and out of the shower. Maybe this morning she absolutely didn't care if I had a chance to shower before school or not.

I stood and began to pace. Did I dare go into the hallway? What if she was in her underwear again? I felt like a prisoner in my own room.

On the other hand, maybe she was giving me the silent treatment—and maybe that treatment extended to not knocking on my door.

I was being ridiculous. I threw on some clothes. I'd just go into the hallway and if the bathroom was free, then I'd take my shower. I headed for the door and saw a slip of paper on the floor.

Bending down, I picked it up. It was from Robin.

Went to school early. See you there.
—R

She must really hate me, I thought, *if she fled the house at the crack of dawn just to avoid walking to school with me.*

Then an even more depressing thought hit me.

What if she and Richard arranged to meet early at school? Maybe they talked all night on the phone and she fell madly in love or something.

I suddenly realized that I had no idea how Robin felt about Richard. Maybe she'd liked him on the date. Maybe she was ecstatic that Richard asked her to the social.

What a mess I was in. Richard wasn't interested in Robin that way.

Now all I'd done was set her up with a guy who wouldn't ask her out again!

Her whole plan would backfire on her, all thanks to me.

Ugh! Why couldn't Robin have been a guy!

Fifteen

Robin

I WAS INCREDIBLY relieved when the first bell rang, signaling the beginning of the school day. I'd been hanging out in the school yard for the past hour in order to avoid having to walk to school with Kit.

As cowardly as it was, I simply could not face him. He wanted me to be what I couldn't be, what I absolutely loathed.

As I headed toward the building, I rounded the corner, and there was Brooke. The only person I wanted to avoid more than I wanted to avoid Kit. I stiffened when I recalled Brooke's nasty words from yesterday. But I knew I had to get beyond them. I'd no doubt see her at Kit's now and then. Right now, though, I wanted to ignore her, but durn my Texas upbringing. I just held my head up high and walked past her. "Howdy."

Inwardly I cringed. I'd meant to say something sophisticated like, "It's so wonderful to see you this bright and cheery morning." I imagined she thought *howdy* was about as hick as a person could get.

But then, what did I care what she thought.

"Robin!" she called out after me.

Against my better judgment, I turned and faced her. Let her toss out her insults. I'd just catch them and toss them back.

She looked really uncomfortable as she approached me. It was a strange sight to behold.

Then she cleared her throat, and her cheeks burned a dark crimson. "About yesterday," she began. "I'm really sorry for the mean things I said. I was jealous of a girl living with Kit, especially an exciting American, but then late last night I realized how stupid I was to be insecure about you, given how unexciting a foreigner you are."

"Thanks," I responded. "I'll take that as a compliment."

She gave me a funny look, then said, "I guess Kit's taking you to the social tonight."

She obviously thought I'd just fallen off the turnip truck and was trying to bait me. I chuckled. "Of course not. He's taking you, isn't he?"

At that moment Brooke looked like a feather

would knock her to her knees. "Kit broke up with me yesterday. Didn't he tell you?"

Correction. I'm the one who could have been knocked off her feet with a feather. Baffled, I shook my head. "When exactly did you break up?"

Brooke rolled her eyes. "After you went storming out of the house. He defended you, said you were so funny and so interesting and so kind." She waved her hand in the air. "Whatever. I stopped listening after a while. I'm surprised he didn't tell you."

I was too, but right now I felt like a cat had gotten hold of my tongue. Why hadn't he told me that he'd broken up with Brooke? And he'd done it before our argument in the gazebo.

"So who are you going to the social with?" Brooke asked.

"Richard," I told her.

She stared at me. "Incredible," she murmured.

I didn't know what to say. "So if you're not going with Kit, who are you going with?" I asked.

"I'm going alone," she snapped. "Not that it's any of *your* business."

Just before creative-writing class, I saw Kit in the hallway. He looked incredibly glum as he put his books in his locker.

I quietly came to stand beside him and leaned against the locker beside his. When he slammed his locker door closed, there I was. I could tell he was taken aback by my presence, which gave me the advantage.

"Why didn't you tell me that you broke up with Brooke?" I demanded. I couldn't believe how forlorn he looked. It actually hurt to see him looking like this.

"My breaking up with Brooke is my business and has nothing to do with you," he said in an incredibly clipped and British voice.

"You're wrong there, buddy. It seems y'all broke up because Brooke insulted me and you defended me," I pointed out.

Kit shook his head. "I broke up with Brooke because I don't have the feelings for her I'm supposed to. And I have those feelings for someone else. Or had them."

"Who?" I insisted.

Kit shifted the books in his arms and looked at me like he was searching for something he'd lost. "The girl I'd glimpsed in you when you were trying to hide who you were. That girl. But that girl doesn't exist, does she?" he asked hollowly just as the bell rang.

No, she didn't exist. *Or at least I don't want her to exist,* I thought as I followed him into the classroom.

I dropped into my seat, suddenly dreading the oral presentation more than I thought humanly possible. I pulled out my copious notes and my well-thought-out and written presentation. I'd printed it out using the printer in Mr. Marlin's office—in the dead of night when I was certain Kit was already asleep so our paths wouldn't cross.

But now the words on paper kept swimming in front of my eyes. I couldn't focus on them. Mrs. Lambourne was explaining the reason behind having us bare our souls, but I really wasn't listening.

I couldn't stop thinking about what Kit had said in the hallway. He had feelings for me? More than brotherly feelings? How could he possibly like that girl? She was loud, brash, pushy, goofy, not afraid to speak her mind, and had the worst Texas twang of anyone alive.

I turned around slightly and stared at Kit. He wouldn't be giving me any thumbs-up encouragement today when I gave my presentation. I remembered how he'd stuck up for me at the Tower of London when the snotty guard had made his Disney World comment. For a heartbeat I'd been myself, and he'd made me laugh. I thought about how I'd revealed my true accent later that night—and he'd sat beside me and we'd talked, really talked, for the first time.

And I remembered last night. When he'd held me while I bared my soul to him. He'd seen the real me then. He hadn't gotten angry until I'd asked him to help me get rid of that girl.

I turned back around. I missed that girl. The real Robin.

A little smile played at the corners of my mouth. I liked that girl too. And so did a lot of other people. Just one guy didn't, one guy who didn't deserve me.

"Miss Carter? Miss Carter?"

I snapped out of my reverie. People were looking at me and smiling indulgently. I figured everyone had pretty much guessed that I'd been daydreaming.

"Miss Carter, it's time for you to give your presentation," Mrs. Lambourne announced.

My presentation. I stared at the papers strewn on my desk. My well-thought-out, rehearsed-to-death, boring presentation. With a deep, shuddering breath I got up—and left the papers behind.

I walked to the front of the class. I wished that I had something to stand behind, something to hide a portion of myself. Mrs. Lambourne had said that speaking made us vulnerable. Speaking the truth would make me even more so.

I cleared my throat, met Kit's gaze, and began.

"My goal for this year is . . . to appreciate who I am, where I come from, and to be myself." Twang echoed around me. Out of the corner of my eye I saw Brooke's eyes widen. She was probably mortified to realize she'd spent time with a true country girl.

"I wanted to come to London for a year so I could turn into a sophisticated, demure girl. But a girl who has pet pigs, loves mud runs, won the hog-calling contest, and can outeat any cowboy in a baby-back-ribs contest isn't meant to be quiet and sophisticated. She's meant to be who she is."

Kit's mouth had dropped open, and he was staring at me intently. Not a good sign. But I couldn't turn back now. Besides, it felt good to finally reveal the real me and not to worry about my twang or my harsh voice or my ability to shove both feet into my mouth at the same time.

I took a deep breath and persevered. "My goal this year is not to be ashamed of my roots. Kit asked what my daddy does, and I told him he was into agriculture. Actually, he's a farmer. And me, I'm a farm girl. I get up at five-thirty in the morning to milk the cows before I leave for school. I also raise pigs and enter them in the county fair. I bought two pigs just before I left. I named them Jar Jar and Binks. I really miss them."

A couple of the kids laughed, but I didn't feel like they were laughing at me. They were laughing with me. If only Kit would. But he was just watching me with those intense blue eyes of his.

"I do have one last goal. I don't want to change so much as I want to learn how to talk to people better. See, on the farm there's just me and my animals, so I spend a lot of time talking to my mare, my cows, my pigs, my dog—and to be honest with you, they're not great conversationalists."

The whole class laughed then. Well, almost. Kit looked like he was on the verge of puking. Not that

I could blame him. I was revealing some pretty heavy stuff here.

I gave everyone a nervous smile. "I can pretty much say anything I want to my dog and he'll just lick my face, even if what I said is totally lame. So I want to learn to be me but around people. I figure if my pets like me—"

The bell rang. Thank goodness, because I knew I was starting to ramble.

To my surprise, a bunch of people clapped. Brooke rolled her eyes. No surprise there. And Kit . . . Kit just grabbed his books and stuff and headed out of the room without even giving me a backward glance.

Guess he didn't like what the real Robin sounded like after all, I thought miserably.

By the end of the day it seemed that the whole school had joined the YAS fan club. Only now people weren't just asking me questions. They were really talking to me.

They thought my life on the farm sounded great, and they adored my accent. Adored my twang. Knock me over with a spring breeze. Who would have thought that the thing I hated most was what would appeal to them?

"Robin?"

I turned as two girls approached me in the hallway. Bridget and Karen. They were in my creative-writing class.

"That was a marvelous presentation you gave

this morning," Bridget announced excitedly.

"Smashing!" Karen added. "I'm going to redo mine tonight. I actually lied about my goal."

I almost asked her why she'd done that, but I knew. It was just plain hard to make yourself vulnerable that first time.

"We're here on scholarship," Bridget explained.

"We actually live on farms in north England," Karen clarified. "We could really relate to what you said today."

Farm girls! I'd had no idea that someone just like me was sitting in class with me.

"Just like you, we felt like we had to hide where we came from," Karen continued.

"But now we realize how dumb it is to feel that way, thanks to your presentation," Bridget told me.

I smiled warmly. "It took me a while, but I finally realized it was dumb too. That's why I decided to speak so openly."

"That was incredibly brave," Karen commented. "You're an inspiration."

I wanted to laugh. I hardly felt like an inspiration to anyone, least of all myself, as I headed home. For all their kind words and enthusiasm for my presentation, I realized that I'd never get it right. I'd never be the kind of girl that any guy wanted.

Now that I'd exposed my true self, I was certain Richard wouldn't want to take me to the social.

And Kit's hasty retreat had made it perfectly clear that the real me sounded awful.

Sixteen

Robin

O N THE OFF chance that Richard had not yet heard about my debacle at school, I absently got ready for the social. It was possible that even if he had heard what the real Robin was truly like, he might still show up. And if he hadn't heard, he was gonna find out pretty durn quickly.

It wasn't a formal affair, but I did think jeans would be out of place. I selected a denim broomstick skirt, a red shirt, and a denim vest with Texas wildflowers embroidered down the front. And what was denim without cowboy boots? I thought about plopping on my hat but decided I didn't want to overdo the Texas image. If Richard was gracious enough to keep our date, I didn't want to send him screaming into the night as I put away my sophisticated image.

Although I had this vision of Brooke racing up to him and laughing uncontrollably about the girl he had really gone out with yesterday. Not that I was able to concentrate much on Richard and Brooke.

My thoughts kept turning to Kit.

It was incredibly obvious that he was avoiding me. I'd been unable to find him after school, and he had failed to join Mrs. Marlin and me for our afternoon tea.

A knock sounded on my door. My heart jumped. Maybe it was Kit. Maybe he just needed some time to adjust to the real me. That was perfectly understandable and cool with me.

But when I opened the door, Mrs. Marlin stood there, smiling warmly. "Your date's downstairs."

Unexpected relief hit me. At least Richard had shown up. Once he got a load of the real me, it would probably be the last time his shadow ever darkened Mrs. Marlin's threshold.

"Give me a minute to see if I can make this hair behave," I told her as I hurried back to the mirror.

Mrs. Marlin followed me into my bedroom. If she noticed that I was talking differently, she didn't say anything. "Well, I haven't much experience fixing daughters' hair," she said wistfully, "but I'll give it a go."

She took the brush and somehow managed to make the rebelling strands that wanted to poke out like rowels on spurs fall back into place.

I captured her gaze in the mirror and smiled. "Thanks."

When I turned, she gave me a big hug. I had needed that so badly that I almost cried. I didn't know how I was going to undo the disaster that this year was promising to be.

On my way down the hall I looked longingly at Kit's door and wondered if he was in there. If he wasn't taking Brooke to this social, then I figured he wasn't going. It would be the first time that I went somewhere without him there to offer me support and encouragement. But he'd wanted to see the real me. I'd warned him that he wouldn't like what he saw.

And yet, even though it had cost me his friendship, I knew that I wouldn't take back my presentation if I could. For the first time since I'd stepped off the plane at the airport, my stomach wasn't knotted up and my palms weren't sweaty.

I was me. And it felt good to be me again.

At the top of the stairs I came to an abrupt halt. Mrs. Marlin patted my shoulder. "There's your date," she whispered before hurrying down the stairs. She squeezed my date's shoulder before disappearing into the living room.

My date. Richard wasn't standing there. I stared in utter astonishment.

Kit stood there.

He wore khaki pants, a blue polo shirt that

brought out the shade of his eyes, and a navy blazer. And the warmest smile that I'd ever seen.

I was incredibly disappointed that Richard had decided to bail out. I'd really hoped that my true confessions earlier hadn't turned him off completely.

But I was so overwhelmed and grateful to Kit for stepping in. I honestly couldn't have asked for a better brother. I knew how he felt after my presentation. His hasty exit had made it abundantly clear. He didn't like me, but here he was, where he'd been from the moment he approached me at the airport—at my side, offering his support.

My heart rolled over, and I wished I could be the kind of girl who would appeal to him. But since I couldn't be that, I could be a good sister.

"Slide down!" he ordered.

I stared at him. Huh? I cast a quick glance at the banister. I'd been dying to slide down it since I got here.

"Come on," he prodded. "You know you want to."

It seemed my brother knew me all too well.

I hopped onto the banister, scooted to the end, and then shoved off. *"Wheeew!"* I cried out as I slid all the way down.

Kit caught me, and I held my breath. It felt so right to be here in his arms, gazing into his mesmerizing blue eyes, studying the way he smiled.

Very slowly he dipped down so I could straighten and my feet could touch the floor.

But his arms didn't leave me. They just moved lower until they circled my waist. I swallowed hard. "Where's Richard?"

"He's at the social with the girl of his dreams . . . Brooke," Kit explained.

Huh? So I had been right. Richard had been looking at Brooke more than a guy with no interest should. I nodded. "Guess I can't blame him for asking her after I revealed my true colors at school today."

Kit shook his head. "Your presentation had little to do with his decision to take Brooke. Actually I prodded, cajoled, and pleaded with Richard to ask you to the social because I knew how important it was to you to impress a 'proper English guy.'"

"I can't believe you did that!" I blurted out, trying to work my way out of his hold.

But his arms tightened around me. "Let me finish!" he insisted.

I stopped squirming. The only time I'd ever heard him yell was at the gazebo last night. He didn't strike me as someone who got upset often, but I sure seemed to put that side of him to the foreground.

He chuckled low. "I'm looking forward to you freaking out on me a lot this year, but right now, I want to talk."

161

"Okay," I said reluctantly.

"After creative-writing class today, I ran out to search for Richard so I could tell him that I didn't want him to take you to the social after all, that I wanted to take you. Richard was very relieved, especially when he heard that Brooke and I had broken up. Richard admitted he had a major crush on Brooke and was dying to ask her to the social. Which, I just learned, he did."

Kit was silent for a moment, and his brow did that cute little furrow. Then his hold on me loosened.

"Blast it all! I just realized that I might have acted way too hastily. Because maybe you like Richard and wanted to go with him. Maybe you don't want to go with me." He stepped back and slapped the heel of his hand against his head as if he was trying to knock some sense into himself. "Maybe I was way out of line—both in setting up your date with Richard and then undoing it!"

I laughed. I couldn't believe this was happening or that he would have such doubts about my feelings. I stepped forward and wound my arms around his neck. "It's amazing how keeping your real feelings to yourself ends up doing so much damage!"

"Don't I know that," he murmured as he slid his arms back around my waist. "I learned that lesson well enough."

I smiled warmly. "I couldn't be happier that you acted hastily. Because it worked out perfectly."

Kit lowered his mouth to mine and kissed me slowly, provocatively. My knees grew weak as my arms tightened their hold around his neck.

He drew back, his gaze holding mine. "I can't wait to spend this year with the real Robin Carter, the one who has pet pigs and won the hog-calling contest."

I groaned. "I still can't believe I admitted that in my oral presentation."

He kissed me again, a kiss as warm as a Texas summer.

I was breathless by the time we stopped kissing, breathless and so incredibly happy. And a little afraid that he would come to his senses.

"I'll be leaving at the end of the year," I reminded him.

"But we'll have the year," he said, "and who knows? Maybe I'll come to the States."

I hugged him. "My parents have a spare bedroom," I murmured. "I've always wanted a brother."

His laughter echoed around us. "Then you'll have to find someone else because there's no way I'll ever be able to think of you as a sister again."

When he kissed me this time, he left no doubt in my mind.

Epilogue

Robin

"YEEHAW!" KIT YELLED just before the mechanical bull sent him flying into the pile of hay.

Standing outside the corral that was inside the Texas Diner, Brooke, Richard, and I laughed. Kit had heard about this restaurant in London and suggested that we give it a go. Right now, I figured he was wishing he'd kept the place a secret. He slowly got to his feet and limped over to us. He rubbed his backside.

"I cannot believe Texans actually do that," he muttered.

"They don't do that," I pointed out. "They stay on the bull!"

Richard laughed loudly, and Kit glared at him. "Let's see you do it."

"No problem," Richard said before sauntering over to the bull.

Kit stepped out of the corral and slipped his arm around me. He moaned. "I won't be able to move tomorrow."

"Tell me where it hurts," I insisted.

He gave me a sly grin and pointed to his lips. Reaching up, I gave him a sound kiss.

We heard a yell and jerked apart. Richard was sprawled on the floor. He gave Kit a sheepish grin before working his way to his feet.

Brooke planted her hands on her hips. "Do you know how embarrassing it is for me that my boyfriend can't even stay on a machine for a single second?"

Richard jerked his thumb over his shoulder. "You want to give it a go?"

"Yeah, Brooke," I prodded. "Why don't you give it a go?"

She gave me an icy look, but it wasn't as chilling as the ones she'd given me three months ago. Ironically, we'd become good friends.

"I'll do it if you will," she dared.

Boy, howdy. She thought that she was going to get out of it. "Reckon you didn't know that back home they call me dare-me-to-do-anything Robin."

She rolled her eyes. "I was only joking."

"Too late!" I snapped. "Climb on the beast."

She did that familiar flip of her hair, roll of her

shoulders, but I could see the excitement brewing in her eyes. She really wanted to do this, but she had to pretend it was beneath her. She straddled the saddle on the mechanical bull and looked at me. "What do I do?"

"Just hold on for eight seconds!" I yelled right before the guy manning the bull pulled the switch.

Poor Brooke didn't last half a second. Her scream nearly shattered my eardrums, and her sophisticated backside landed hard in the hay along with her pride. Somehow she managed to get up elegantly, and she walked stiffly out of the corral. "Let's see you do it, Miss I'm Having a Hard Time Holding Back My Smirk."

"Aww righty," I drawled. I turned to Kit. "Kiss me for luck."

He obliged in a very warm way. Durn, I loved his kisses.

I sauntered toward the mechanical bull and threw my leg over the saddle. I grabbed the saddle horn and raised one arm in the air. I gave a sharp nod. "Do it!"

The bull bucked and turned, but I just let my body become fluid with the motions. It wasn't as easy as riding a horse or chasing pigs, but it was easier than trying to be something I wasn't. I'd learned a lot in the last three months. Mainly that I was the most interesting person these people had ever met. How small town was that?

The buzzer sounded, and the bull came to an

abrupt stop. I hopped off and gave the guy manning the bull a salute. I strolled cockily over to my mates, blowing on my fingers before buffing them on my shirt.

Kit creased his brow. "How did you do that?"

"Very successfully," I assured him.

He narrowed his eyes. "I'm going to give it another go."

"Marlin! Party of four!" the hostess called out.

I slipped my arm around Kit's. "Later—I'm starved right now."

We were escorted to a table covered with a red-and-white-checkered tablecloth. After we sat, the hostess—who wore Western garb—handed us the menus. I opened mine, settled back in my chair, and figured I was gonna eat more tonight than I had the entire time I was in London. My mouth started watering as I looked over the selections.

"Brisket?" Brooke murmured cautiously. "What is brisket?"

I looked over the top of my menu. The corner of her lip was curled up. I almost told her that I'd expected her to learn the cuisine of a country before she ate in its restaurant, but I knew too well how hard it was to know every little thing.

"Beef," I supplied, and went back to drooling over the menu.

I heard menus slap closed. I looked up.

Everyone was staring at me. "Y'all know what you want already?"

Kit shook his head. "Why don't you order for us?"

"All right," I said, really getting into the fact that I was in my element and they weren't. Who would have thought this would be so much fun? "I reckon we ought to get a sampling of everything and share."

"Share?" Brooke echoed. "Isn't that a bit much, even for friends?"

"This isn't a fancy restaurant, Brooke. You're gonna eat them baby-back ribs with your fingers," I pointed out.

Brooke rolled her eyes in disgust, and Kit laughed heartily. "I can't wait to see that."

I leaned back, queen of my domain. "I figure y'all need a good sampling of Texas fare, so we'll have baby-back ribs, brisket, pulled pig, potato salad, coleslaw, baked beans, corn bread, and lots of barbecue sauce. Then we'll move on to blackberry cobbler and apple pie."

I didn't think I'd ever enjoyed eating so much. Who would have thought that eating barbecue would make my friends look as clumsy as a three-legged calf? And talk about messy! They couldn't quite figure out how to get all the barbecue sauce off their face and fingers. I thought it was great!

After we ate, we went to the dance floor.

"Are we going to line dance?" Richard asked. "I've heard of line dancing."

"Not if you're getting a true taste of Texas," I explained. "Texas guys like to hold their girls close."

As if to prove my point, George Strait began crooning "I Cross My Heart."

Kit took my hand and led me to the center of the dance floor.

He smiled warmly at me. "So teach me how they dance in Texas."

I stepped close and put my hands on his shoulders. "Just put your hands on the small of my back and take small steps. I'll follow wherever you lead."

I fitted my head into the crook of his shoulder as we began to sway slowly in time to the music.

"Having fun?" he asked quietly.

I nodded and twined my arms more firmly around his neck.

"I love you, Robin," he whispered near my ear.

My heart did a little do-si-do, and I leaned back slightly to meet his gaze. "I love you too."

He smiled warmly and lowered his lips to mine. I could smell straw and barbecue. I heard the heartache of country music. I felt the thudding of Kit's heart keeping perfect rhythm with mine.

He'd heard my twang, my outspoken ways, my brash outbursts—and seen me freak out too many times to count.

And he still loved me. Small-town, farm-girl Texas Robin.

My parents were going to be here in a couple of weeks, and they planned to stay for a month. I couldn't wait to show them my school, introduce them to everyone, and take them around London.

I knew my daddy would be proud of me: He was going to see the same old Robin he'd sent to London. Only maybe now I was a little smarter.

Do you ever wonder about falling in love? About members of the opposite sex? Do you need a little friendly advice but have no one to turn to? Well, that's where we come in . . . Jenny and Jake. Send us those questions you're dying to ask, and we'll give you the straight scoop on life and love.

DEAR JAKE

Q: *My grades aren't so great, so my parents won't let me go out on "school nights." I'm not even allowed to hang out with my friends after school. I have to come straight home and do my homework. Forget that! How can I make my parents understand that friends are more important than grades?*

TR, Mandeville, LA

A: You heard it here first: Friends aren't more important than grades, and grades aren't more important than friends. What *is* important is that you find a way to balance all major aspects of your life. Your grades, your friends, your relationship to your family, extracurricular activities, your job, hanging out, whatever. When one is seriously suffering, like your grades, it's time to focus on that. Balancing your time isn't easy, but neither is summer school!

Q: *How do you know when you're ready to do more than make out with a guy? My boyfriend says he's getting tired of just kissing. I'm afraid he might break up with me. What should I do?*

KA, Charlotte, NC

A: Here's the thing: Doing something you're not ready to do will make you feel as miserable as being dumped by your boyfriend. So don't do it. I know it's hard to stand up to pressure, especially when you really like or even love the guy. But it's even harder to deal with how bad it feels to betray yourself.

Q: *My best friend and I are both trying out for the lead in our school play. It's a really tough situation. If neither of us gets the role, we'll probably stay friends. But if one of us gets it over the other, won't it break up our friendship?*

MC, Fair Lawn, NJ

A: Only if both of you allow it to. You're right: It is a tough situation. And it will require the two of you to care more about your friendship than the role itself. Remember—if you get the role, you'll want her to be happy for you. So if she gets the role, be happy for her. Maybe you two can sit down and talk over the possibilities— and agree to support each other, no matter what.

Q: *I have a huge crush on a guy in my English class. Problem is, he's sort of a nerd. He's nice and funny, though, and I think he's so cute. I asked my friends what they thought of him, and they said he was a total geek. So I guess I can't like him, right?*

PR, Trenton, NJ

A: It's more like you have to choose. If you choose your friends' opinion, then you don't get the guy. If you choose the guy, then you might have to deal with your friends ragging on you. So which is it going to be?

DEAR JENNY

Q: *My younger sister, Lisa, does whatever she wants and never gets in trouble. If I so much as put the wrong fork in the wrong spot when I set the table, my mom yells at me. It's so unfair! Why does she get special treatment?*

AS, Springfield, IL

A: The best person to answer this question is your mom. What she has to say might surprise you. Perhaps your sister is going through something right now that you don't know about; maybe she needs to be cut a little slack. Or, maybe your mom doesn't realize that she's coming down hard on you. Let her know how you feel.

Q: *Why do my parents make such a big deal about my clothes, hair, and makeup? They comment on everything! I'm so sick of it. My mom thinks I wear too much makeup, and my dad doesn't like my clothes. They want me to dress the way they do: boring and old. How can I get them to leave me alone?*

BB, Arlington, TX

A: Rolling your eyes and telling them it's your

life probably won't accomplish what you want. I suggest talking to them straight: Tell your parents that you like the way you look, that you feel comfortable, that the way you present yourself expresses who you are. Let them know how much their criticism hurts your feelings. They might not ever like the way you dress, but they might start to accept it.

Q: *I'm totally in love with a guy in my math class. He doesn't know I'm alive, of course. I'm not popular or part of his crowd—there's no way he'd ever like me, let alone notice me. But how do I stop my crush?*

KE, Juno Beach, FL

A: There's a great saying that goes something like this: "If you do nothing unexpected, nothing unexpected happens." Give yourself more credit. And never give up on something until you at least *try.* You never know!

Q: *I'm new at my school, and I have no one to eat lunch with. I'm so scared even to walk into the cafeteria that I've been hiding out in the bathroom for my lunch period. But I can't hide forever. What am I going to do?*

DD, Temple, TX

A: I know it's tough to be the new kid, and even tougher to face an entire cafeteria when you don't know a soul. The good news is that kids are pretty friendly and understanding. Look for an empty seat, walk up to the table, and let the people sitting there know that you're brand-new and don't know anyone. I'll bet they invite you to sit down. And, you'll make some new friends right away.

Do you have any questions about love?
Although we can't respond individually to your letters,
you just might find your questions answered in our column.

Write to:
Jenny Burgess or Jake Korman
c/o 17th Street Productions,
an Alloy Online, Inc. company.
33 West 17th Street
New York, NY 10011

Don't miss any of the books in *Love Stories*
—the romantic series from Bantam Books!

SUPER EDITIONS

TRILOGIES
PROM

BROTHERS

YEAR ABROAD

Coming soon:

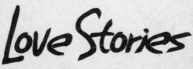